CAREGIVERS
AND OTHER STORIES

Raymond M.E. Aguirre
<u>Circa Sunshine Press</u>
2021

For Christina, Phoebe, and Kristoff
To whom I dedicate all the blood, sweat, and tears
of my labor.

FOREWORD

Dear reader,

In 2015, I wrote a book. I did not have grand ambitions for the book, other than to quell an ever-increasing itch to say something. I was not sure what I wanted to say, but I knew I had to say it. Fast forward a few months later, I ended up with a short story that would turn out to be my first book, *The Hill: A Novelette*. You will find that entire story, as well as its accompanying flash fiction piece, *Toro*, in this book.

My book never received any critical acclaim. Apart from relatives, friends, and a few other people, *The Hill* was unknown to the world-at-large. It was unequivocally a commercial failure. And yet to this day, I am thankful for having written that book, because it yielded something that no amount of recognition could match. It liberated me. It introduced me to a voice I did not know I had or could muster. Best of all, it allowed me to free myself of all the internal conflicts and emotions I had as a young immigrant from the Philippines. Because of *The Hill*, I was able to gather the courage to write all the other stories within this book, a few of which have been published.

For a time, I thought these stories were the beginning of something, the seeds for a possible foray into a full-fledged literary career. Whether that could have been true is something I would probably never know. All I know is that life took me in a completely different direction, and I had to shelve these stories until now.

Now, for a variety of reasons, I am once again hit with the strong desire to continue writing. I initially considered sending these stories out for publication, but I decided against it when I realized what I really wanted out of them now. It is not recognition I am after, but the chance of start over with a blank slate. So while these stories are as meaningful to me now as they did when I wrote them, I feel that directly sharing these stories to the public will provide me with the closure I need to explore new possibilities as a writer.

I hope that these stories will give value to your life as they have to mine.

-Raymond M.E. Aguirre

Table of Contents:

CAREGIVERS
(Originally published by
The Left Coast Review in 2016)

I have told you
everything you need to know
in all the things
I never said.

I am sitting next to Leila as she slept on her side. Strands of her hair are in picturesque disarray. Her shoulders are snuggled under the covers, and her eyes never flicker. It is almost as if she is feigning sleep, as if secretly waiting if I am going to say or do anything that might explain why, in the last few weeks, according to her, something is "different" about me.

I brush my hands through Leila's hair in the darkness of my apartment, which I had recently moved into after I got a new job as a LVN at a rehab in Pasadena. Leila works in a nursing home nearby, and we had met because I was introduced to her by a fellow nurse.

I kiss Leila softly on the lips and begin to speak.

*

It was Ronel who got me the gig as a caregiver. After he got fired at the fast-food place where we used to work, this was the kind of work he did. The job was easy, he told me, and it was good money. Plus, he had free board and weekends off. There was nothing else to ask for.

For two years, he had been a caregiver for this old man named Dwight Harper, who had Alzheimer's Disease. Ronel lived with Mr. Harper and Mr. Harper's family in their beachfront townhouse in Huntington Beach. Life was good, Ronel said. All Ronel needed to do was escort Mr. Harper to the bathroom, dress him, feed him, give his medications crushed in applesauce, and make sure that Mr. Harper did not injure himself.

The old man had a habit of wandering, which was why he needed 24-hour monitoring.

Somehow, my boy managed to impress Mr. Harper's family. When we used to work at the fast-food joint, Ronel was the poster child of fuck-upness. Eddie, our ex-manager, was always on his ass for all sorts of things. But somehow, Mr. Harper has remained in one piece under Ronel's care.

Ronel hooked me up with a family who knew the family of Mr. Harper. He said I would be caring for an old woman, 90 years old, frail, and who had just had a massive stroke. The old woman also had Alzheimer's Disease and had started to become combative towards caregivers in the last few months.

I took the job, not even knowing what the hell I was about to get into. Ronel easily convinced me with a few keywords: "easy", "good money", "free board", and "weekends off". My boy made it sound like fucking paradise.

On my first day, Ronel went with me to see the patient and her family. It was also the first time I had seen Ronel in about a year. He had changed somewhat. His hair was now brushed neatly on one side, and he talked differently. He was still the same fool that I had known, but he had toned down from his days at the fast-food joint when he would greet friends with profanity and chest bumps. He still smoked weed but had cut down. Said he couldn't get through workout sessions if he was killing his lungs. Whatever happened to Ronel, I sure felt obsolete, a Luddite whose ways and views on the world-at-large had become so irrelevant to the new Ronel.

Anyway, Ronel introduced me to Mrs. Belmonte, the daughter of my patient. Mrs. Belmonte toured me and Ronel around the house while she briefed me on what was expected. She said she needed help, because even though Mrs. Belmonte lived with her husband and her daughter, all three of them were out of the house often. Mrs. Belmonte also said that she would have kept her mother in the nursing home had the administration not found a clever way to push her mother out.

"Nobody wants a high-risk, combative patient on Medi-Cal," she said.

The last stop of the house tour was the room where my patient stayed.

"Nita," Mrs. Belmonte said. "Nita is my mother's name. You can call her Nita, Ms. Nita, or *abuelita.*"

Ms. Nita was sleeping when we came into her room. She slept most of the day, which meant I could nap around too, Mrs. Belmonte said, as long as I was not a dead sleeper. Then, Mrs. Belmonte said that Ms. Nita needed a diaper change every two hours and must be repositioned side to side. Repositioning Ms. Nita was of "utmost" importance because she had a "big sore" on her back. I was also told that a nurse would come in every two days or so to provide wound care. Just before we left Ms. Nita's room, Mrs. Belmonte asked how much of a stomach I got for that kind of stuff. I said I had a lot.

My orientation was smooth sailing, all in all. The only awkward part was when Mrs. Belmonte asked if I smoked, a question which I hesitated to answer but answered honestly anyway. She said yes, I could smoke, but only in the backyard and only if I didn't leave butts around the house. And, if I could possibly quit soon.

After the tour, Mrs. Belmonte asked me and Ronel to sit in the living room. It was there that we hashed out the details of my employment--my pay, my days off, my living arrangement. $200 per day, Saturdays and Sundays off, free housing for as long I stayed with the family.

Deal. I could start next week.

*

I had been working three days when I first met Ms. Nita's home health nurse. I was in the middle of diaper change when the nurse rang the doorbell. That day, Ms. Nita was running a temperature and was having a bad bout of diarrhea.

I told the nurse about it and the nurse suspected she had *C-Diff.* I knew nothing about what it was, other than the fact that Ms. Nita's stool stank and looked like the week-old lunch I accidentally left beneath my car seat a couple of weeks ago.

"Samuel, by the way," I said, as the nurse began to examine Ms. Nita.

"Please to meet you," she said. "Natasha." Natasha had this dry tone, which left no hint as to where her vulnerabilities might lie.

Under the circumstances, neither of us thought about shaking the other person's hand. Natasha began to carefully peel away at Ms. Nita's soiled wound dressing while I held onto Ms. Nita on the opposite side. She was getting heavy, so I decided to distract myself by fixating my eyes on Natasha's scrubs which had a logo of the Philippine archipelago. It was little loose too, so it sort of exposed her bra. When Natasha began to notice where my eyes were wandering, I turned away and pretended to scratch my nose.

"*Saan ka sa atin?*" I asked.

Natasha glanced at me with a blank stare.

"*Cavite,*" she replied, coldly. She was intent on looking at Ms. Nita's pressure ulcer.

"I see...," I said.

Natasha asked Ms. Nita if she was in any kind of pain. She had already asked her several times before this, and each time Ms. Nita just mumbled in her stupor. Natasha spoke with Ms. Nita in such a sweet voice, nothing like how she spoke to me.

"Listen, do you mind handing me the Hibiclens? I'll hold on to Ms. Nita for a sec," Natasha said.

"Which one is that?" I asked.

"The blue plastic bottle. It'll say Hibiclens. You can look through my bag, it's OK."

I dug through Natasha's bag and fished out the bottle, which was tucked at the bottom, past the surgical scissors, the gloves, the paperwork, the countless sachets of topical medications. I had hoped to see something I could comprehend in this heap, something to small talk with Natasha about. Something like...I don't know. A picture of her poodle or something.

After I handed the Hibiclens to Natasha, I reclaimed my post holding Ms. Nita on one side. Then, I started staring at Natasha again, but this time, my eyes were a little elevated in order to avoid her bra. Surely, she was from the motherland. She had streaks of blonde in her hair and a pair of blue contacts. But I could tell very easily if somebody was an immigrant *pinay*. I had never been wrong. Natasha's accent kind of gave her away too, although she had probably been in the United States long enough because she had lost some of it.

When Natasha was through with the wound treatment, we covered Ms. Nita with a fresh set of blankets and positioned her pillows properly so she would stay turned towards the window for the next two hours.

"When will you be coming back?" I asked.

"On Friday," Natasha replied.

Normally, at that point, I would have already pulled out something from my bag of tricks. My shamelessness in soliciting a phone number, my lousy jokes. But something about her intimidated me.

"I'll see you on Friday," I said. And due to the circumstances, we never got around to shaking hands.

*

Every night, I would sleep in a twin bed next to Ms. Nita. Or at least I tried to get some sleep. Often, I would go into a stupor only to get shocked out of it by Ms. Nita's voice. She garbled random stuff in Spanish all the time, and soon, I started to learn a little of her language. *Dios mio!* and *Dolor! Dolor!* had become part of my vocabulary.

Whenever Ms. Nita got agitated, I would rub her back gently and tell her it was all going to be OK. Then I would peep into her diaper to see if she had emptied herself out or something. Often, she would be wet to the bone, and I would have to change sheets in the middle of the night. It drove me crazy in the beginning, and I even told Ronel I was not cut out for this shit, and thank you for the job referral, but I would be quitting the next morning.

By then, I had sort of developed an understanding of what might had happened to my boy Ronel, why he had become the strange man I could almost not recognize. Being a live-in caregiver can make you bat shit crazy. It was like solitary confinement on steroids.

Nevertheless, I stuck with my job, though not for any noble, altruistic reason. Ms. Nita was a cash cow. I mean that in the least offensive way, but she was really a cash cow. I got $1000 per week under the table, which meant I didn't have to share my spoils with the government. And although I had the weekends to myself, I was too exhausted to do shit. I never had so much money and so little energy to spend it.

And then there was Mrs. Belmonte and her family. Mrs. Belmonte could get picky, short-fused, and generally terrifying, but boy, did she keep the house running smoothly. She helped whenever she could, and she paid on time. She remembered my birthday and made me eat dinner with the family. She and her husband worked at JPL, the rocket lab in Pasadena. They tried to explain to me once what they did, but I never understood. All I knew was that anybody who had anything to do with rockets had to be madly intelligent.

The daughter of the house, Elisa, was rarely present. She was only 17, so her parents rationalized she was just going through a phase. Elisa hated her family, though. I knew this from a conversation we had some months ago, when I caught her smoking a joint in the backyard. It was past midnight. She was wearing white jeans and her hair was braided. Her facial features were strong but like Michelle Rodriguez strong, and her curves were unbelievable.

Anyway, we somehow ended up laughing at nothing under the moonlight that night, until I realized it was time to reposition Ms. Nita. Elisa kept following me around even though I told her I wanted to keep my job badly. But she kept on following me and patiently waited in my twin bed while I took care of Ms. Nita. When I finished, she pulled me in, and we started to make out.

"Are you sure about this?" I asked.

"Well...you know what they say about girls in white jeans," she replied.

"I don't."

She whispered sheepishly to my ear, sounding embarrassed by my own ignorance. That night, I added "*Damelo por el culo, papi*" to my Spanish vocabulary.

*

After a year of caring for Ms. Nita, we ended up going to Methodist Hospital in Arcadia. Septic shock, the doctors said. Ms. Nita was hooked onto

IVs at the hospital for three days. Not to sound like a jerk, but I liked being in the hospital more than I liked being in the Belmonte house. Being in the hospital meant I didn't have the comfort of my twin bed, but it also made me feel like I had just emerged from a well after 10 years of submergence. Seeing other people had suddenly felt like a new, magical phenomenon.

My human interaction at the Belmonte house was limited mostly to Elisa. Since that first night, Elisa and I had been fooling around more and more. Having sex next to Ms. Nita had become somewhat of an extreme sport only Elisa and I knew about. When Mr. and Mrs. Belmonte were around, she pretended to not even recognize me. The Belmontes were pleased that Elisa was home more often.

Anyway, after those three days at Methodist, I was told by Mrs. Belmonte that we would be going to a nursing home to continue Ms. Nita's antibiotic treatment.

The one we went to was this nursing home in Santa Anita. We got there at around three in the morning, so it was quiet.

The only person that met us-us meaning me, Mrs. Belmonte, Ms. Nita, and two EMT's-was this nurse named Sachiko, who told us she was the supervisor. After introducing herself, she told the EMT's to cart Ms. Nita's gurney to the North Station, to Room 19A.

"Ms. Nita, she will be your nurse," Sachiko said, pointing to a woman typing intently onto a computer. "Her name is Natasha."

Now, if this were another story, one that would pass as a fairy tale, I would say that this second encounter with Natasha was destiny. That I had unknowingly played into the hands of the universe and that we were, after all, star-crossed lovers.

But that was not the case. In fact, I never saw Natasha again in the whole time that Ms. Nita stayed at the nursing home. She worked per diem because she had other jobs like her home health route. What really made this chance meeting with Natasha somewhat significant didn't really have much to do with Natasha herself. What made this night significant was Ms. Nita. Ms. Nita, who was oriented X0, who had succumbed almost completely to dementia.

Ms. Nita had been mute the whole time she was in the hospital. She never ate, as hard as I tried to feed her. The whole time, Mrs. Belmonte had pestered the nurses and the doctors to evaluate her and to decide if it might be time to put a feeding tube on Ms. Nita. At the hospital, Ms. Nita never even wailed in pain at night. And she never screamed for *Pancho,* her late husband. She had also been asleep most of the time at the hospital and was asleep when we arrived at the nursing home. She was like basically dead.

But as if Ms. Nita sensed something in the air, she opened her eyes the moment Natasha stood from her seat and welcomed us to the facility.

"*Usted es tan bonita*," Ms. Nita said. Then, she smiled at Natasha, a face I could tell she knew, but whose name she cannot remember.

*

Ms. Nita had been a day laborer when she was young, imported from Oaxaca by the United States government under the Bracero program. Mrs. Belmonte said Ms. Nita was a firecracker back in the day, a vocal advocate for immigrants especially during the 50's, at the height of Operation Wetback. Mrs. Belmonte showed me pictures of Ms. Nita standing side by side with Cesar Chavez and this Filipino labor leader, Larry Itliong.

Raised by a single mother after her father got hitched with a longtime mistress when she was five, Ms. Nita made it a point that she and her daughter would marry right. Ms. Nita taught Mrs. Belmonte all about love, about its dangers and its beauty. Ms. Nita said that love was something best left to the brain, not the heart.

Mrs. Belmonte told me all this one night as she and I were basically watching her mother die. The antibiotics were not kicking in as expected, and her infection grew worse. She was now hooked on oxygen 24/7 and had been poked so many times she had developed these big bruises on her forearm. The therapy department stopped giving her exercises and she did not eat much of anything anymore. Whenever I repositioned her or changed her diapers, the smell of her pressure sore made me more nauseated than ever before. There had been talk of Ms. Nita going on hospice, but Mrs. Belmonte was on the fence with that idea. Hospice was essentially a death sentence, Mrs. Belmonte said.

Even Elisa started to visit Ms. Nita in the nursing home, something she had never done until after a month of Ms. Nita's confinement.

"She's a strong woman, your grandmother," I said, when Elisa came by one day.

Elisa did not say anything. She did not even bother to look at me. She ran her hands through Ms. Nita's hair.

"*Abuelita*, I have something for you," Elisa said.

Ms. Nita was snoring, and her eyes were fluttering.

Elisa pulled out something from her bag. When I saw what it was, my chest dropped.

"She will be just like you," Elisa said. "And if he turns out to be a boy, I know he will be the bravest of them all. Just like you."

Ms. Nita continued to sleep, gargling on her phlegm.

Then Elisa looked at me. She raised the pregnancy test to where I could see it. It had two lines. "What do we do now?"

In hindsight, I should have probably prepared a better response, something with more of a heart.

Instead, all I said was, "Are you sure it's mine?"

*

Ever since Elisa's mind fucking revelation, I feared not only for my job, but also for my life. I began to imagine that Mrs. Belmonte would show up at the nursing home in a rage and chop my little ass into bits and pieces. Or, if not that, a couple of cops with a warrant charging me of statutory rape.

The thing is you never really want to get caught in this kind of shit just as things are starting to get better in your life. As Ms. Nita declined, my compassion for her grew. I began to see my job not just as a way to cash in every two weeks, but as a privilege. The woman could well be a national hero. As time went by, I learned to stop *needing* to be on Ms. Nita's side. I started *wanting* it.

Three months passed before I heard anything about Elisa. She had decided to run away without a word; no note or whatever to explain to the Belmontes what was up. All they knew was that she had asked them for some money for a trip to San Diego with her girlfriends one night and the next morning she was gone. Mrs. Belmonte asked me if I knew anything about what might have happened, and, of course, I said I did not.

I wondered how long I could keep my lies, and if I should just come clean and get it over with. I thought about all the places where Elisa might be, but I guess I screwed her more than I talked to her. I realized I really knew nothing about the girl, other than the fact that she was pretty much the only reason I never went completely insane the whole time I was alone in the Belmonte household.

Then, one day, I got a call from a new number. Since I never answered calls that weren't identified by my caller ID, I let it go to voicemail.

"Hi, Samuel, this is Natasha Severin. I was Ms. Nita's home health nurse. Call me back as soon as you can."

I called back. It rang twice before somebody picked up.

"It's me," the voice said. "Elisa."

"Listen, where are you?" I asked.

She wasn't listening.

Instead, she broke out into a speech, as if she had a script hashed out for this phone call. She talked about how she was not mad--not anymore, at least--and that if I wanted to, we could talk. She said it was up to me if I had the balls to take any responsibility for the baby, and if not, I was free to do so. She could get by on her own. She had, after all, Ms. Nita's blood running through her veins.

I wish I could tell you that I saw this as a moment of salvation, a chance for me to set things right. I wish I could make you see that I was not a bad man. That I was a man.

Instead, I said, "I can't Elisa. I'm sorry." Then I hung up.

Several nights later, Ms. Nita died. Mrs. Belmonte had already decided some days ago that she did want Ms. Nita to go on hospice after all. Mrs. Belmonte signed paperwork saying that should Ms. Nita become unresponsive, the nurses should just let her go. *DNR,* in other words. No chest pumps, no intubation, no transfers to the acute hospital. Just comfort measures. Ms. Nita had earned the right to die in peace, Mrs. Belmonte concluded.

I stopped working for the Belmontes, of course, and never saw Elisa again. On my last day, just before Mrs. Belmonte handed me my last paycheck, she said, "Thank you for everything Samuel. You are a great caregiver. I hope you find yourself a new, nice family to take care of."

*

Leila is still asleep. Every few minutes, she would stir, but would remain unaware I was sitting by her side. I look at her, tuck some of her hair behind her ear and say, "Believe me when I say this: I am not who you think I am. For your own good, love anyone but me."

__CHAPTER SIX__

(Originally published in Issue 5 of
The Mulberry Fork Review in 2016)

The secret to life
perhaps
is making all kinds of mistakes
until you have exhausted every
avenue
to fuck up
and the only thing you can do
is get things right.

It was dark already when I made the trek back to Los Angeles from Sacramento. Once in a while, I would see the outlines of trees and crops partly illuminated by the moonlight and the headlights of the vehicles on the road. Mostly though, all I saw were the bald plains of Northern California. I was cruising down the 5 South. I let the wind in--chilly, but soothing. I smoked yet another cigarette and let its stench graze my battered car seats, my shirt, and the nice air outside. I turned up the knob on the stereo and searched for the rock station. I sat back as Metallica played For Whom the Bell Tolls. Then, I allowed myself to slouch back a little and turned on the cruise control.

Every few minutes, I would look at the passenger seat, at a small envelope that was sitting on it. I beamed silently with joy each time I looked at that envelope. It contained a document stating that I can now work as a licensed vocational nurse. This was it, I thought--a new life.

Two hours ago, I had phoned my girl Mimi to inform her of the news while I wolfed down my one-man celebratory dinner at a KFC in Stockton. She shrieked like I never heard her shriek before and congratulated me. I also called Terry, Mimi's co-worker, and the staff developer at the facility where I had been planning to work. He said he would speak with Rowena, the director of nursing, first thing tomorrow morning to tell her that I could finally start working. The only person I did not call was Mama, whom I thought deserved to hear this good news personally.

*

October 26, 2013. I was in the middle of Maternity Class when Mama called me.

"It's your father," she said. "Come now. We need you. We're at the Queen of the Valley ER."

When I got there, Mama was bawling. *Tita* Odette, Papa's older sister, made it there before I did and was trying to console my mother. At first, I took Mama's panic with a grain of salt because she was the hysterical type, the type that overplayed things, but I also acknowledged that things were not good. Papa had been admitted to the hospital twice over the last three months for a slew of heart issues.

"One more," the doctor warned during the second admission, "and he could be a goner."

Papa was a withered mess when I saw him that night. He was nowhere near the pompous corporate executive in Manila that stood beside President Fidel Ramos and Senator Juan Ponce Enrile in a photo that hung in our living room. His face, which in the last few months had already sagged, sagged even more. His entire body also sagged, and if he sagged just a little more he would liquefy and just drip off the bed.

He died at 4:32 A.M. of the 27th, with Mama wailing by his side, and *tita* Odette and the rest of my Papa's siblings crying softly in the background. I stood quietly during this whole procession, debating between sadness and anger.

In the years that we had been in the United States, Papa was beset by bad luck. After he had a falling out with his business partner in the Philippines, we moved to the United States, hoping that things would pick back up in his career. Instead, he spent years being limited to minimum wage or temp jobs or sometimes, being unemployed.

Despite his luck, however, Papa stayed idealistic.

"One day," he would always say. "We will live a better life. This is America! The Land of the Opportunity!"

Papa was pretty much the only person in the family who never told me to become a nurse. He never dissuaded me from becoming one, but he had told me plenty of times never to be a nurse just because it was a safe bet. He knew that I never imagined myself a nurse. That I preferred the solace and the empowerment writing afforded me.

"Finish that damn book of yours already," he'd always say, fully aware of how many years I'd been trying to revise a manuscript that I kept in my closet. It was a young adult novel about the struggles of an 18-year-old immigrant, which I started writing the day we arrived in Los Angeles.

After his funeral, I looked through the pages of this book. I considered adding to it, an entire chapter perhaps, but realized I had run out of things to write about. Little did I know that as the lines blurred between my life and the difficult world in which my protagonist lived, it would become much harder to write.

Mama changed since Papa's death. She liked to clean, but Papa's death made her clean even more. She was always mopping and scrubbing something. It was as if she was hell bent on trying to erase every bit of Papa's remnants within our apartment.

At night, she kept the television on, even though she had always been the one most concerned about our electricity bills. She did not cry as much as I had expected her to, though she was usually serious. I thought her lack of emotion was strange, since Mama had never really been the stoic type in times of uncertainty.

A month after Papa died, Mama and I realized we had little money. Money had been a problem even when Papa was alive, but his death gave the issue a bit more urgency. I had to work more. Mama had to work even more. More than what her body could sometimes bear, in fact. Her migraines troubled her more often, and I had no way of keeping track of how many Tylenols she had taken. Eventually, Mama and I decided we had to make do with a small room in La Puente, a downgrade from our one-bedroom apartment in Covina.

I worked part-time at a Filipino fast food in West Covina and full-time at a warehouse that provided the stock and the supplies at that fast food place. Meanwhile, Mama cashiered at a Filipino supermarket in the same complex, washed dishes at Denny's in Pomona, and sold Moringa herbal pills to her friends in her spare time. We were too tired to do anything besides work, but we made OK money together--enough to pay for a roof, enough to pay for a banged up Civic, enough to breath. But still, there were plenty of nights when I would look up at the popcorn ceiling, wondering if we could do better than this.

Often, Mama would make remarks about this neighbor or that friend of a friend who was a nurse.

She'd tell me that these people were doing great, that I should consider becoming one, and that it was not too late to shift from creative writing to nursing. She had been trying to persuade me to become a nurse even before I went to college, but when Papa died, she became more persistent. I tried to resist the idea, to hold on to what idealism Papa had encouraged me to have.

But after a while, I had to give in. The urge to rise from poverty overpowered every bit of will I had to live the life of an artist.

One day, I gave Mama a nice surprise when I said, "Yes 'nay, I'd like to go to nursing school. I quit writing."

*

I left the house at four in the morning, got to Sacramento around noon, and left at around four in the afternoon. I spent an hour or so walking near the state capitol trying to contain my excitement and ended up posting some cheesy status on Facebook that said, "All the hard work has paid off." When I got past Stockton, I lost my signal, and did not get it back until I got to Fresno. By then, I already had 102 likes. Of course, I could have waited for my license in the mail and avoided this long road trip, but after waiting close to two months, I could not wait any longer. I decided to take my chances and travel to NorCal myself.

I got back to West Covina fifteen minutes to ten and decided to go to The Heights. While I smoked, I listened to my voice mail. I had three calls. One was from Mimi asking where I was. Another was from

Mama asking me where the hell I was and why all her calls went straight to voicemail. And then the third call was from Terry asking if I wanted to drink.

I texted Terry to say I was too beat to drink. Then, I called Mama to tell her what I had done that day, that I meant to deliver the news to her in person, that yes, I was safe, that I'm sorry I didn't let her know I drove to the opposite side of California to get my nursing license, and that no I won't do this kind of thing ever again. Mama responded by crying over the phone, telling me how good of a son I was. After that, I called Mimi and said I was on the way to pick her up.

We ate dinner at this 24-hour Pho place along Cameron Ave. They had lousy Vietnamese soup, but they were open 24/7 and they had an open veranda to sit at late at night. It was the perfect place to smoke and eat while the rest of San Gabriel Valley slept. I volunteered to pay.

Mimi glanced at me with pride and amusement and said, "Sure, Mr. Big Shot Nurse."

I kissed her on the cheek. There was no way I would let Mimi take the tab on our dates again, ever.

"So, Rowena said she'll see you in the morning," Mimi said.

"Can't wait," I asked. "Is it a full-time position?"

"Not right now, but just hang in there."

I kept looking at her.

"Don't worry about it," she said. "You know how some of the people at the facility are like. Sancho looks like he's the next candidate for the Fly-by-Night Nurse Award."

"Well, don't you think I'd be like Sancho?"

"You won't Sam. I know it. You'll do great there."

I nodded and gave myself credit. I did ace nursing school, to my surprise and to the surprise of Mimi and my mother. I took almost all the awards during graduation, with the exception of the Perfect Attendance Award.

After dinner, we checked in at Elegant Heights Inn, which I paid for as well. It was a motel by the freeway owned by this Indian family. For the last three years, we had been frequent flyers at that joint. We liked Elegant Heights because it was cheap, but it didn't look cheap. I mean, the sheets didn't smell like cum or looked like somebody had just been boned on it. It was at that motel where I would always promise Mimi of a better life. Where I would always vow to make something out of myself, out of our lives.

And that night, after we had fucked, and after she had burrowed herself in my arms, I slept knowing that I had finally kept that promise.

*

Four months after Papa died, Mimi and I were at the housewarming party of Jen, this 40-year-old RN that Terry was fucking around with. Their relationship was supposedly a covert operation--known only to me, Mimi and this other LVN named Joe. I never understood why their relationship had to be a secret, since most of the staff was *tsismosa* and *tsismoso* and already knew what was up. But Terry and Jen continued to keep things hidden, as if secrecy were some type of fetish they had.

Jen was already piss-drunk by the time we got to her house. Mimi and I got there pretty late because she had worked the 3-11 shift and had a fall incident 15 minutes prior to endorsement. I picked her up from work, like I always did, because it was the least I could do.

Anyway, when Jen saw me, she glanced at me through her half-open eyes and gave me this over-the-top welcome hug. She normally never said hi to me, at least not directly, and at least not when she is drunk. Jen had this annoying habit of referring to me in the third person even when I was present. Like, for instance, we would be in the same dinner table--me, Mimi, and Jen--and Jen would be like, "So what does Samuel do for a living?" I hated that shit.

After chatting with Mimi, Jen staggered across her living room and crashed into the couch. Terry was equally fucked up beside her, with a half-consumed bottle of Patron dripping on his scrub pants. Later on, they would disappear, like they always did.

I helped myself to a beer in the kitchen, while Mimi started talking with her co-workers in the living room. I didn't mind. Joe came hollering out of nowhere and said some shit I did not understand. He was high on something, I'm sure, but I couldn't tell what. He approached me, gave me a chest bump, and then we helped ourselves to some food, which had gone cold by then.

Mimi looked back at me from her little circle. I knew that look. I hated that look. It was the look that said, "Sam, I wish you could be part of this conversation. I wish you could be one of us."

"I'm OK," I said. She didn't hear me, but she read my lips and nodded. From where I stood, I could not hear what they were talking about. The volume of the electronic music and the voices of the other drunken nurses were too loud. I did not bother to come closer, because I knew I would not understand a thing they were talking about anyway.

The party raged on until about four in the morning, and by then I was about as fucked up as every single person in the house. However, I somehow managed to be the last one awake. Mimi was on the floor with a blanket up to her neck, snoring. Jen and Terry were nowhere to be found. Everybody was littered all over the living room, like casualties of an apocalyptic event. It was a housewarming alright, because the house felt like a hundred degrees.

I had been to many nights like these. It was during these nights when Mimi and her co-workers dissociated themselves from their profession--from the heavy weight of carrying other people's lives on their shoulders and the paperwork that came with such responsibility. I attended these parties because of the free booze and because of Mimi, but also mostly because they were the only events where nobody looked at me strange whenever I said I wanted to be a writer, where I did not feel like I had to defend myself.

Before I slept, I decided to look around Jen's house. It was a beautiful three-story house that had hardwood floors and new furniture. It was a place Papa would have loved, a place I could have never bought with two minimum wage jobs and a writing career that was going nowhere.

At around noon, Terry woke up and suggested we go someplace far. We ended up driving to Primm, Nevada. Mimi and I decided to tag along because she was off and there was nothing else to do. Joe and this nurse aide Mikhail also went and brought some leftover alcohol with us. We all drank on the way to Nevada. We laughed and laughed.

While they continued to laugh, I stopped at one point. And it was during that moment when it seemed like a switch had just suddenly gone off in my head. I looked outside the car window and bathed in the sunshine that passed through it. It was a beautiful morning, hangover notwithstanding. I looked at
Mimi, Terry, Joe, and Mikhail. And for the first time, I did not see a bunch of nurses trying to find an escape from their tough job. Instead, what I saw were people who were so satisfied, so relaxed, so complacent about life. They all looked like they had reached a transcendent state of mind, a state of mind that I thought, albeit erroneously, I was only going to achieve as a writer, and a state of mind that I could not afford on my current salary.

When I saw this, I thought, "I'm sorry Papa, but I think it's time to let that book go."

*

I was up and about early the next day. Terry had left a voice message saying Rowena wanted to see me at nine. I was at the facility by 8:25. I refused to smoke with Terry because I didn't want to stink when I met with the Boss.

The interview was short, shallow, and pretty much a formality. Terry had everything arranged before I got there.

Why do you want to work here? Because I am passionate about helping people and I believe this is the best place to exercise that passion.

Are you good with people? Absolutely.

Do you have a habit of calling off work? No ma'am.

What shifts are you available? I am open to any shift.

We start new grads here at $20/hour. Is that OK with you?

Of all my answers, my agreement with the hourly pay was the one that I thought about the least. I had meant all of my answers, but man, twenty bucks was good. I ran calculations in my head and realized that working full-time both at the fast-food place and at the warehouse would not even equal what I was about to make as a nurse.

I smoked with Terry after the interview and then decided to hang around the facility.

"Welcome dude," he said. "Welcome to St. Martha Convalescent Hospital." I sat inside Terry's office looking at the people outside.

An old woman wheeled herself in front of us and started to turn the bathroom knob. She set off the alarm that was attached to her and Terry bolted out of his seat.

"Ms. Cherry, please," Terry said in such a phony, sweet-ass voice. "Please don't get up by yourself. I will call your nurse if you'd like to go to the bathroom." Terry then called out a nurse's aide and gestured towards Ms. Cherry. Then, he came back to his office.

"That's Ms. Cherry dude," Terry said. "Been here for eight years. You'll get to know her more when you start working. She's a fall risk, a little confused, but she's really sweet."

I watched as Ms. Cherry was wheeled by the nurse's aide into the toilet. She looked thin and frail. Her arms were marked with purple discolorations all over. I wasn't sure how the staff could hold her, even gently, and not break any of her bones.

After a half hour of sitting around, Terry decided to have me do some paperwork. After that, he toured me around the facility. He got approval from Rowena to pay me for four hours that day.

"80 bucks for just fucking around," I thought. "How can I complain?"

Terry introduced me to the staff, which was 75% Filipino. There was *tita* Lucy in the North Station, who was old and was munching on some peanuts while charting. She stared blankly at me for a brief moment, nodded, and immediately went back to charting and munching. Next, there was Jill, a cute little *chinita* that reminded me of Yolly, my hot date for junior prom. Terry and I hung around her station, the West Station, for a little while until we saw Mimi approach us.

"How was it?" she asked. "How did it go with Rowena?"

"Ah! You know he'd get it," Terry said. "No doubt about that."

Mimi squealed and hugged me. Then I backed off a little. Just to keep shit professional and all.

Afterwards, Terry continued to introduce me to the other people. There were many, and soon, my mind started to float as I met several other LVN's, CNA's, RN's, and administration staff. One of the people I met was this stern-looking woman whom Terry introduced as the medical records director.

"She will be your new best friend," Terry said.

"Medical records will be on your ass with audits, especially if you are new. Don't get frustrated. Use it as a learning experience."

I nodded. I looked all around me to see everyone so busy. Call lights buzzed here and there. People walked in and out of rooms. Phones rang from all directions. A woman somewhere screamed "fuck you!" while Rowena bandied about with a stack of papers looking for Lucas, the admissions director. Ms. Cherry was by the front door trying to get out, which set off the alarm to the whole facility. I took in this whole picture, this chaos, and prepared myself for what was about to come.

*

Three months passed before I got acclimated to the whole nursing home routine. Sancho ended up quitting a month after I came on board, so I did end up getting a full-time position on the 11 P.M. to 7 A.M. shift.

During these early months, I became literate in talking about incident reports and other kinds of nursing documentation. I experienced firsthand what hell my nurse friends had to go through just to write these things. I had my fair share of falls and skin tears and orders from Rowena to rewrite my documentation on them to make them seem like they were not facility's fault even though they clearly were. I also learned how to send a patient out to the hospital for various bogus illnesses so that he or she can come back to the facility days later with renewed Medicare coverage. I had also become used to telling Ms. Cherry not to go to the bathroom by herself about 200 times per shift. I also experienced getting yelled at by doctors, getting harassed by department heads, getting guilt-tripped into covering for absent nurses almost every night, and having sleepless nights because I could not stop worrying whether I had mistakenly drugged some poor old man or woman to death. Then, I came to know many of the faces Terry introduced to me on my first day, the people who would have been something else in life or was former this or former that in the Philippines, but who had to make do with being a LVN or a CNA because there were no other jobs out there other than nursing.

I took all this in, considered these experiences as initiation rites to the nursing profession. During this time, I never wrote, partly because I was always too drained to do so, but mostly because I had refused to see its worth. I began to see it as a waste of time, an ancient pastime that only served to hold me back from fulfilling my promise to Mimi and my desire give a better life for Mama.

It wasn't until eight months after I started working at St. Martha, a week after Rowena was on my ass for yet another issue on my documentation, and a day after I was ordered by management to send out Ms. Cherry to the hospital under the false pretense of a bladder infection, when I wistfully cracked open the pages of my novel. For a second, I thought I heard Papa's voice saying, "Finish that damn book already!" Then, I wondered, what Papa would have said if he knew what I had been up to lately. The book felt ancient in my hands, like a volume of spells that trapped hordes of damned creatures within its pages. I began to flip through the book and took my time in doing this. I relished each line that had once felt so natural to write, but now sounded like the voice of an unknown person. And then, I wondered as I looked at the last sentence on chapter five, the last chapter I had written, if I still had it in me to write the sixth.

<u>PRIMETIME</u>

For all your chaos
you will always
still be
the one I love.

8:15 PM. I am sitting with Leila in her living room, half-awake, numbing my mind with today's re-run of this game show on *The Filipino Channel* called *Afternoons with Joey!* Today's episode shows a woman crying her eyes out, both from utter joy and from the pressure of being faced with a life and death decision to risk all her winnings for a bigger prize or to take the 100,000 pesos worth of cash the game show host is dangling in front of her eyes. Most nights, after a long day at the bread warehouse, there is nothing to do but watch stuff like this.

Leila grabs my hand, shrieks softly to herself, and awaits The Big Decision.

The woman makes a brash decision to risk it all. The television audience gasps, holds its breath. Joey Santillan, the game show host, the god of Philippine noontime television, begins to pull out a cardboard from inside a box that the contestant selected just minutes earlier. Joey pulls the cardboard in such a slow motion it is almost painful to watch.

"Gloria," Joey says, "You can walk home right this second with a hundred thousand pesos, but you chose not to. If this is the wrong box...well...are you willing to risk it?"

Gloria continues to cry, holding her hands up to her mouth.

She's still going for the big prize.

Joey continues to slowly pull the cardboard out of the box. Leila is leaning towards the television now and almost falls off the fucking couch.

She does not notice me pick a flake of dandruff from her hair.

Suddenly, Joey plunges the half exposed cardboard back into the box. I feel the on-air crowd release its tension, like a long-held fart. Leila falls back onto the couch.

Meanwhile, I see a small roach on the floor. It is one of many that troll the walls, floors, and crevices of Leila's apartment in Eagle Rock, which she shares with her parents and seven other siblings. I contemplate the roach's fate. It is walking in a broken pace, as if hesitating, as if looking out for its dear life, as if wary of a foot out of nowhere that might squash it into a mush.

I let the roach go. It shall live another day.

*

Leila hails from *Sitio Maharlika*, a small *barangay* in one of the northern provinces in the Philippines. When she was small, she played by the river, which was just below the house where she lived. Leila told me that *Sitio Maharlika* was a vibrant town, a town that thrived on the noise of the *talipapa* that was just a block away from her house, the children that never seemed to stop playing in the streets, and the *sunog baga* that played cards, smoked cigarettes, and drank San Miguel beer in the *sari-sari* stores every single night.

But Leila said that things always got noisier than usual every time election season rolled around. Her town, like most poor towns, was a favorite campaign stop for many politicians. Growing up, Leila had brushed hands with the likes of Joseph "Erap" Estrada, Fernando Poe Jr., Bong Revilla Jr., and Tito Sotto.

Every election year, Leila and her family would gather on the streets with the rest of the townsfolk while the presidential candidates and their party list paraded and handed out all sorts of care packages to the masses. Leila said that the politicians would always roll into town in a convoy of floats, like muses vying for a grand prize in a pageant. They always came dressed down, sleeves rolled up and all. The people of *Sitio Maharlika* loved them and always welcomed the politicians like heroes-- like salvation. Especially those that had careers in the entertainment industry. It is not unusual for action stars, comedy stars, drama stars to transition to politics in the Philippines. The more film or TV credits, the better. Regular politicians do make the cut too, but their odds of election success are better if they show willingness to perform a dance number or sing a song at a campaign rally.

Leila's mother, *Manang* Pacita, the *sanggano* of the town, the one that even drug addicts and drunks did not attempt to fuck with, mistrusted the transient politicians that came to *Sitio Maharlika*. She'd say things like, "Oh these fools! Look at them pander to the poor! Children, do not believe a word they say!" But every election season, *Manang* Pacita would take her kids to see the politicians and encourage them to grab whatever goods they could get.

*

Joey is now standing next to Gloria, a middle-aged woman with short hair and a baggy shirt that said, "*Afternoons with Joey!*" Joey has his arms on her shoulder and the microphone to her mouth.

Joey begins to ask about *Nanay* Gloria's life while glancing at her husband, who is in the audience. The camera pans to a man about *Nanay* Gloria's age, who is sitting in the lower bleachers of the studio set with his hands clasped together. He looks teary-eyed as well. A melancholy background music is played as *Nanay* Gloria reveals on national television how her husband, *Tatay* Tonio, had just been cut from the bakery where he worked. He and *Nanay* Gloria are struggling to survive on the meager income they are getting from her job at the shoe factory.

Joey expresses his sympathy on-air.

"I feel sorry for her, *mahal,*" Leila says. I can see that she is about to shed a tear.

"*Nanay*, in addition to 100000 pesos, we will add a *sari-sari* store package with your prize," Joey says.

The crowd claps and cheers. To them, Joey is a savior. A godsend. Possibly God himself hiding behind the veil of a noontime game show host. People seem to have this belief that *ye who come to Joey will be blessed with abundance.* I personally think it is a load of shit, but what the hell do I know? No wonder he is being touted as the top prospect to become president in next year's elections, a position for which he had publicly expressed no desire to run for, but for which he had constantly hinted interest with the press. The camera pans back to the stage, to the left of *Nanay* Gloria and Joey. A replica of a tiny convenience store is revealed by two *morenas* in midribs with glitters and short pairs of skirts. They are moving their hips seductively. The store package is sponsored by Purefoods.

Camera pans back to Joey and *Nanay* Gloria. *Nanay* Gloria is ecstatic, convulsing with tears of joy. She looks overwhelmed by this outpouring of blessings, seemingly unable to process luck of this magnitude. Joey thanks Purefoods.

Another roach walks past me again. Its skin is of a different shade, so I know this is not the one I had seen earlier. This time, I step on the roach for no reason. I imagine the other roach I had spared, if maybe it was related to this one. And if roaches knew how to feel enough anguish to know the meaning of revenge.

Joey says something funny, or at least something that is supposed to be funny. I must have dozed off for a second because I did not hear what Joey said, although the subtle look of embarrassment on *Nanay* Gloria's face tells me that the joke was at her expense. Joey does this all the time with all the contestants. But *Nanay* Gloria is a good sport and tries to laugh out loud with the crowd.

Out of nowhere, Joey asks *Nanay* Gloria if she has any kind of talent. She tells him she can dance. The crowd urges her for a "sample".

The fact that this show has been on for three years means the ratings are good.

The studio goes dark, and the spotlight is on *Nanay* Gloria. She takes center stage. First it is quiet. And then, *Twerk It Like Miley begins* to play, its volume progressively increasing as *Nanay* Gloria starts to get warmed up. She ends up doing this awkward dance for a good fifteen seconds before the lights come back on. Joey is now laughing his ass off.

"OK! OK! I think we've had enough of that," Joey says, shaking his head in utter disbelief. The crowd is laughing. *Nanay* Gloria grins, pretending to be oblivious of the embarrassment she had put herself through.

The game is on again. This time, the stakes are higher. Joey raises the grand prize to 115,000 pesos in addition to the *sari-sari* store package. Joey asks *Nanay* Gloria if she wants to keep going.

Nanay Gloria looks scared again, about to cry again. Camera pans to *Tatay* Tonio, who is gesturing that he wants his wife to keep going. *Nanay* Gloria decides to keep going. Joey shrugs and begins to pull the cardboard out of the box.

A zero peers out from the box. Leila is sitting forward again, squeezing my hand. We are trading sweat. I sweat because I naturally do. She sweats because little things excite her, something which I love about her, for whatever reason.

Another zero appears. We are five digits from finding out if the cardboard contains a million pesos or a string of seven zeros.

Joey plunges the cardboard back into the box. He puts his arm around *Nanay* Gloria's shoulder again. He pretends to count the cash in his hand. Then, he calls one of the mid-ribbed girls to hand him another wad of cash.

"Last chance, *Nanay* Gloria. 125000 pesos. And a *sari-sari* store!" Joey says. "*Saan ka pa?!*"

Nanay Gloria is silent, clutches her hands to her mouth.

"If you keep going, you could get 1 million," Joey reiterated. "Or you could go home with nothing."

I think of the roach I had spared and the one I had killed. I can feel that a coordinated roach attack aimed at me is going to happen.

Joey begins to pull the cardboard out of the box once again. Three other zeroes appear. It is 8:39. *Tanging Ikaw* will be on any minute.

*

I was 12 when the second EDSA Revolution happened, 14 years after the first movement that threw Ferdinand Marcos out of office. I watched on TV as the reign of ex-action star-turned-president Joseph "Erap" Estrada's regime crumbled under the weight of the people's might. Every night, my father would give us a long-distance call from Los Angeles, where he had been an OFW when I was little, just to check up on us. He knew everything that was going on, because he had a cable subscription to *The Filipino Channel*, the same channel that now features this piece of shit show hosted by Joey Santillan. My father told us not to go outside, to stock up on canned goods, and to be prepared in case shit got bad.

I kind of knew what was going on but was not old enough to formulate an elaborate opinion on the whole thing. All I knew was that everybody seemed to be chanting "Erap resign!" and that Senator Tessie Aquino-Oreta was now supposed to be regarded as a *pokpok* for being caught by news cameras doing this dance in the Senate hearing minutes after she and other Erap loyalists succeeded in preventing access to a crucial piece of evidence that could have incriminated Estrada. The energy of the citizenry was so profound during this time that I was moved to make little banners at home that called for Erap's resignation.

I took part in the second EDSA Revolution by waving my banners passionately in front of the television, despite having no damn clue what I was fighting for.

*

Nanay Gloria continues to have an internal debate as Joey tries to rendition *Nanay* Gloria's twerking. The crowd goes nuts with a seemingly orchestrated laughter once more.

"I'll go with the 125,000 pesos!" *Nanay* Gloria says. Joey pretends not to hear anything and brings his ear closer to her.

"That's it! I'll take the 125,000 pesos and the store," *Nanay* Gloria repeats, this time louder.

Joey puts the cardboard back in the box and the crowd cheers. Leila breathes a sigh of relief. *Nanay* Gloria breathes a sigh of relief.

"*Nanay*, I gave you your chance," Joey says. "You chose the 125000 pesos cash prize and the *sari-sari* store package. Now let's find out what you would have won."

Joey slowly pulls the cardboard out of the box again, but a little faster than before. One zero appears. Then two. Then three. Then four. Then five.

"Are you really, really, absolutely sure about this *Nanay?*" Joey asks, plunging the cardboard back into the box.

I excuse myself for a cigarette. Leila nods, but is not paying attention. I check the vicinity for an angry mob of roaches.

When I return, the studio lights are off again. Joey is having a duet with *Nanay* Gloria, and they are singing a song from Joey's latest album. The song is incredulously lousy, some very commercial jingle that had no soul whatsoever. Yet, it had been on the Top 40 in the Philippines for the last five weeks. *Nanay* Gloria, I could see, is in her groove, though her singing is more volume than tone. Joey, himself, isn't doing much of a job either. After the song ends, the crowd cheers, as if they had just witnessed a classical masterpiece. *Nanay* Gloria blushes. Joey makes a joke, but I did not quite get it.

I realize that I am so pained to watch this shit, this so-called "variety game show", so I tell Leila to shut it off. At first, I try to wean her off the TV by necking her, then by trying to make out with her. She's like, "hey what the fuck!", but I have a steel will and stay my course for a minute or so. Finally, she gets mad, and I plunge back into the couch, where I am stuck to watch Joey and *Nanay* Gloria.

I don't know how much time passed, but the next thing I know, *Nanay* Gloria is jumping for joy, crying, and smiling all at once. I look around the house to see if a pack of angry roaches is about to wage war against me. Leila hugs me, and then kisses me on the lips.

"OMG! She won! She won!" Leila says, on the brink of tears.

Nanay Gloria's decision to stick with the 125,000 pesos and the *sari-sari* store package was right. She'd have come out with zilch had she selected the box.

"Maraming maraming salamat po Sir Joey," *Nanay* Gloria says, sobbing as she buries her head on Joey's shoulders. *Tatay* Tonio is summoned to the stage by Joey and is escorted there by the mid-ribbed girls.

Tatay Tonio hugs Joey as well, thanks him to no end.

Joey waves at the crowd, tells them it's an honor to do his job, thanks Purefoods, then tells the crowd to buy his album. Credits roll.

This is the last I will see of Joey until tomorrow's pre-recorded telecast. But I can almost see him in his big-gated mansion in Ayala Heights, walking past his sports cars after a hard day's work, half-submerging himself into his tub that had hot and cold water--which he probably had--simmering in its warmth, amusing himself at the thought Gloria and all the other Glorias that had come before. All of them twerking it like Miley or making a fool of themselves in some other way.

And then I envision him on television years from now, not wearing the garb of a funny game show host, but as a man with a stoic expression running for the presidency or the Senate or something. After all, he's got "the man of the people" image going for him. *Para sa masa,* or something along those lines, would be his slogan. His candidacy would be so convincing that he will actually make everybody believe that he is nothing like those that have come before him--those men and women who had sold their souls while in office--by using places like *Sitio Maharlika* as his podium. Once in office, he will pass several useless laws to much fanfare, learn to dip his hands into the pork barrel, maybe go to trial once all his cronies get bored of him, and then maybe go to jail. Or, if he does not go to jail, he will still most likely end up pissing the Filipino people off in some way, and be regarded as yet another *trapo*, another sweet-talking fool that lulled the citizenry into a sense of false hope. At that point, another "Joey" will come into the public's eye, not necessarily in the form of a game show host, but who will be just as charismatic. Charismatic enough to convince Filipinos that this time, things will be different. That he will not be like those that have come before him.

When that happens, we, the Filipinos overseas, will watch things unfold from the comfortable distance of our foreign channel subscriptions, and have small talk about the happenings in the motherland at somebody's *salu-salo* with an odd combination of nostalgia and relief. Relief in the idea that, despite the trials of *buhay Amerika*, God still ought to be thanked because we had made it out of the country.

Why I am thinking about all this is beyond me.

In any case, I am sitting with Leila, and we are now watching *Tanging Ikaw*. It is about this rich, young man that falls in love with a beautiful chick from the province. As with most soap operas, this one has got a whole plethora of conflicts within its plot, but the main one stems from the fact that the boy's mother is a totally evil *matapobre* who would do anything to keep the chick away. At one point, she even enlisted the conniving daughter of a *haciendero* to seduce the son. Totally primetime material. Leila and I do not know how it will end exactly, but I know it will somehow involve the mother, a role played by Celia Rodriguez, falling from grace, and changing her attitudes. The series will end and another series of pretty much the same ilk will start, starring the latest teen couple and, perhaps, with Jean Garcia as the antagonist.

Another roach peers from underneath the Lazy Boy just in front of me. I don't know if this is the same one I had spared.

The roach lurches forward in a stiff and almost military-like cadence. I remove one of my shoes and raise it up to my shoulder. I braise myself for a full-on war between man and pest, for a band of angry roaches to reveal themselves from under the La-Z-Boy. But no attack materializes. Instead, the roach veers to the left, by its lonesome, towards the kitchen.

I decide to spare it. It shall live another day.

THE BRIDE

They were lost causes
finding purpose
in each other's breaths
with every mile that passed by.

I woke up that morning not knowing where the fuck I was and how the fuck I got there. All I knew was that I felt heavy, like I was cemented to the bed or something. I moved my eyes to see where I might be.

I was in a hotel room, though I had no recollection of ever getting there, and I was alone. It took a couple minutes before I felt my tongue again, and it tasted like booze, cigarettes, and somebody's pussy.

Moments later, the door gave off a soft beep and unlatched. Mimi let herself in. She had a beverage carrier in one hand and a bag of McDonald's on the other.

"Toss me my panty will you?" she said. "I don't get what all this fuss is about you guys going commando. I'm freezing down there."

I was still cemented to the bed, though I somehow managed to feel my fingers. It searched for Mimi's underwear, which was resting on my leg. I held it up to my face and tossed it weakly towards Mimi.

"Heard from Derek yet?" she said.

She pulled down her pants, exposing nothing but her shaven pubis. Then, she slid into her underwear and back into her pants.

"Nope," I said. "I don't keep track of other people's husbands."

Mimi glared at me. We had already spoken about this. I was to keep my mouth shut when the big day comes.

Just then, there was a loud banging on the door. Mimi paused while the banging continued. When

Mimi opened the door, we found Derek leaning on it. He crashed onto the floor and made a loud thud when he landed on the carpet. Lenny, Derek's girlfriend, and Mimi's cousin, was right behind him, clutching a blazer to her chest. She looked like a mess, too, but she had enough energy to reach the bed. Then, she started snoring. Mimi rolled her eyes.

Once I managed to feel my legs, I slowly crept out of the bed. I opened the window and stared outside. We were in Old Town Las Vegas, I could tell, because there was the big dome, the one that transformed into a movie screen every night, the one that played Kiss music videos every night.

"The wedding is at four. You all better get yourselves ready by then." Mimi kicked Derek in the gut, and he *ugh*-ed in his sleep.

I kept staring through the window and started to think.

*

The day Mimi told me she was getting married to Derek, it was too late for me to do anything about it. Not that I had any right to do anything about it anyway. We weren't together, officially. We were just co-workers. We worked in a Filipino-owned bakery in West Covina that was in the same strip mall as a bunch of other Filipino stores and restaurants. Since we worked most days, we saw each other a lot. When the owner wasn't around, we'd smoke cigarettes and make out by the big trash bin behind the bakery and exchange stories about the Philippines. Once, she told me about this church in their town. It was an old church, maybe like a hundred years old, but it was where her parents got married. She told me that it was her dream to get married at that church one day.

"Whatever happened to your fairy tale wedding?" I said, as I tried to make sense of her news about Derek.

"It's just for the papers," Mimi said. "It's not like we'll start living together or something."

She showed me a photo of her and Derek, this white boy that worked at the In-N-Out in Baldwin Park. She said it was one of the many photos they had taken--photos which she was compiling to prove to the government that they were a real couple.

"You're aware you could do hard time for this right?" I said.

"It's for my family," she said. "It's either this or I get deported back. You know I can't afford that. Especially now that *tatay* is gone."

"How much are you paying him?"

Mimi paused. "Well, he asked for 15 grand," she said.

"No shit! That's quite a fortune, girl."

Mimi shrugged. She had been on an expired tourist visa for the last eight months. The immigration people were probably out there hunting her down. Time was running out. But still, I could not believe what Mimi was telling me. This kind of thing was exactly what Mimi and I used to laugh about. We had this smug habit of making fun of the Filipino women who came to the bakery with their white husbands in tow. Behind their backs, Mimi and I would make up the surnames of these Filipino women, which we knew for sure was an odd hybrid of a really *pinoy* sounding last name and a really white sounding last name.

"Well, Mrs. Mimi Katigbak-Johnson," I said.

"Congratulations. I'm happy for you."

"Shut up, Sam," she said. "This is not a joke anymore."

"You're damned right it isn't. Just hope you'd have kept me in the loop a lot sooner."

"Are you being jealous?"

"Should I be?"

"You tell me," she said.

*

I couldn't remember when, but one day I hit up Mimi. This was after I already knew about Derek. I figured I should take her out. I figured that I have messed around her for quite a while--longer than anybody else out there--and not once have I formally asked her out.

We agreed to meet at seven at her place. She rented a room in Lenny's house, which was owned by *Tita* Precy, Lenny's mother. *Tita* Precy was never fond of me. Behind my back, she had called me a *sanggano*, a *tambay* with no future, according to Lenny. While I will never know exactly why *Tita* Precy had a lot of bones to pick with me, my guess is that she did not like me because I was poor, and I did not have any papers. Mimi and I were pretty much in the same boat.

See, I had a fairly simple plan after high school. Mama and I only planned on leaving Manila temporarily for the summer, and then head straight back home to move on with our lives. We never planned on migrating. We were doing fine. Papa, who had been an OFW when I was young, started a business in Manila after several years abroad. He started with his partner from scratch, but the venture flourished over the years. But then, one thing led to another starting that fateful summer and we found ourselves stuck in America until Papa died. With Papa gone, Mama took no more than two seconds to decide that we should stay put. And we had stayed put in America for more than eight years, long after our tourist visas had expired.

Anyway, the night I came to pick up Mimi, *Tita* Precy was the one who opened the door. She did not look happy to see me. When I greeted her, she merely responded by looking at me from head to toe. Thankfully, Mimi had the sense to dress up early, so I didn't have to wait for her for too long. She had on a navy-blue dress. It was one of those I liked a lot, because it did not stand out like the ones she wore to the clubs. She was sparsely made up, too, and she probably did this on purpose. She knew I liked her better when she was plain-looking.

"So where are we headed?" she asked.

"Someplace far," I said.

"Like where?"

"I don't know," I said. "Away." Suddenly, I considered the idea of eloping with her.

Soon, we were on the 10 East. The car windows were rolled down. A whiff of Mimi's cologne grazed my nose, fanned by the wind outside. We were on the way to nowhere, in particular. I really did not have any plans for the night other than to be with her.

Mimi placed her legs up on the car seat. This was one of our few days off. And her car bill was paid. And her rent was paid. And the money for *Kuya* Benjo's leg surgery had also just been wired, along with some capital for *Nanay* Pacita's sari-sari store. As we drove through the freeway, Mimi was wide-eyed, seemingly unable to believe that air could do more than just be still. The thing is, if you work long days and long hours, air is usually not your friend. Instead, air hovers like a heavy cloud, ready to break into a storm at any moment.

Mimi and I considered going as far as New York, but instead, we ended up in Las Vegas. When we got there, we checked in at the Fremont hotel. The sun was peering out of the horizon already by the time we got to our destination. We were beat, but we somehow managed to go through two rounds of fucking and a bottle of Jägermeister. That morning, I watched her sleep. Normally, I'd crash after we fuck. But this time, I had to stay up. I had to see her face. It had changed somewhat, like it was illuminated or something. All of her facial features seemed to have become more highlighted. Her small eyes, her slightly puckered lips, her smooth hair strands that fell smoothly across her face. It was all that beauty should be. I held her face as if it was a delicate artifact from a glorious, ancient kingdom that was now lost to the sea.

*

Fucked up as we were on Mimi's wedding day, we somehow made it to the Office of Civil Marriages by 3:30. I had been nursing a major headache since that morning, even though I had already downed about four Tylenols and slept through most of the day. Derek's eyes were still a little bloodshot, but he did his best to appear groom-like. The folks at the strip mall called him Mr. Pretty Boy, but then again, by the rules and standards of the strip mall, everybody who was not part of a minority group was a pretty boy. Filipinos are sometimes racist like that. Anyway, Mr. Pretty Boy did his best to live up to his moniker. He had a suit and a tie on, and his hair was brushed back, though he had this hunch and these dull eyes that made him look like he was high on something all the time. The girls both wore silk dresses, and they looked beautiful. Meanwhile, I wore a suit that I rented two hours ago and thought that I did not look too shabby. I thought, if I only had papers, this wedding would have been a totally different story.

Mimi stood next to Derek, her arm wrapped around his. She said, "Don't fuck this up, please."

Derek winked. "I got this," he said.

Inside, Lenny and I sat on the chairs while Derek and Mimi went looking for the official that was going to conduct the ceremony.

"Sam, did you ever think about doing what Mimi's doing?" Lenny asked.

"No, not really," I said.

"Well, you should." Lenny rubbed her hand against my arm.

"Doesn't this whole thing disturb you?" I said.

"You mean, watching my boyfriend get married to somebody else? Nope. Not really. I mean, how do you think the husbands and wives of actors manage to live with the fact that their spouses sometimes need to sleep with other people on-screen just to make a living?" Lenny said. "It's all an act, Sam. It's all an act. Most marriages are."

I stayed quiet, unconvinced.

"I'm just saying," Lenny said. "Mimi doesn't have papers, Derek does. You don't have papers, I do."

"I have a bad credit score," I said. "Nobody's gonna want to lend me money to pay you."

"Oh, come on, Sam. You know I love you," Lenny said, laughing. "I'll take IOU's. I know where you live. Plus, you like to screw my cousin. So, it won't be too hard to find you."

Several minutes later, Mimi and Derek returned with the official--a serious-looking, middle-aged, mustachioed man that reminded me somewhat of Freddie Mercury.

As Derek and Mimi positioned themselves in front of the official, I felt a pang of anger.

"If any of you has reasons why these two should not be married, speak now or forever hold your peace," the official said.

I could not believe how taunted I felt by such a standard, ceremonial statement. Lenny gave me a playful elbow. When I looked at her, she chuckled and shook her head. I paid little attention to the rest of the ceremony, which took about five minutes.

The only time I listened was when I heard the official say, "You may now kiss the bride."

After that, I watched as Derek moved his head closer to Mimi, and she moved closer. Then, I looked away, but not before Mimi threw me a quick glance just before their lips touched. It was the look I was waiting for. The look of apprehension. And when I saw that I did not feel so bad anymore. This was all just an act, I thought. This was all just an act.

CANVASSERS

I am a collection of broken
fragments
wishing only you
can piece together.

I. At Work

Some nights are easy. Some are not. Often, they are not. Unless you are like Aubrey, then you would have more of the better nights. But believe me. You will have plenty of bad nights. Ask Aiza, a *kababayan* born in America. Or Attorney Lester Noriega, the man who said fuck you to a six-figure corporate law job in Florida to be a screenwriter in Los Angeles. Or me.

We are called canvassers. In moments of shameless self-importance, some of us proclaim ourselves "activists", "guardians of democracy" or "the modern-day Paul Reveres". We are the nuisance of the common shopper, of the after-five crowd of the mothers and their children that had been so carefully trained not to speak with our kind at any time, for any reason. We brave locked doors and dogs and their sometimes dog-like owners, hoping that our scripted pitches will somehow find its way to a good heart willing to become monthly donors to ACLU or Planned Parenthood.

Tonight is definitely not a good night. The new iPad is out, and Aiza's pitches are falling on deaf ears. I had given up for the night. Six hours in, Aiza and I have collected five dollars. It was from an old man.

"Beer money," he said. And then he told God to bless us. Donnie will definitely be on our ass.

I call Attorney Noriega to see how he is doing, and he tells me to wait a minute. He muffles the speaker, and then cusses somebody out on the other end of the line.

"Fucking hillbillies," he said, turning his attention to me.

"Get a job!" I hear a man yell on other line.

After chatting with the Attorney, I think about the Santa Monica beach which is just across from where Aiza and I are, at the Third Street Promenade, and if maybe Aiza would want to take a dip with me. I ask her to smoke instead. She is a true *pinay* beauty, but her heart belongs to another woman. We get partnered a lot, but we rarely talk. The only thing we have in common is this last cigarette in my backpack that I asked her to share with me.

II. Moving Up

Obama is winning in the primaries. Change is upon the nation, supposedly.

I am also promoted today. My official title will now be Field Manager. There is fifty cents raise to the base pay, in addition to the commission. And then, I also get to work with my "own team". This means I will never work with Aiza ever again because she was my Field Manager.

I earned this useless title after four nights of acquiring at least three $75/month memberships in a row. Seven people lost their jobs today though, including Tosca, this chick that did nothing during work hours but scribble the letter B in her journal over and over again.

I wonder how long I will last. The average worker spends a month or less at this job. I am now on my third.

For today's assignment, I am given somebody to orient. His name is Fin. He is fresh out of college. Or maybe a college student. I cannot remember for sure, but I'm sure he hasn't seen the world, judging by the fact that he believes in life and in the idea that it has something in store for him.

Aiza is partnered with a new chick named Marcela. While Fin is busy giving me more spiel about himself, I imagine Aiza and Marcela getting hot in a dingy toilet.

Fin and I get assigned outside a CVS on Westwood Boulevard. I show Fin the ropes, like how to approach a random shopper without getting pepper sprayed.

"Be casual," I say. "Act like you are talking with a friend. But be confident in your approach. Don't look like you are lurking."

Fin tries his luck. Once. Twice. Thrice. He fumbles on his poorly memorized pitch on all tries. Every one of his uninterested audience respond by politely excusing themselves and then walking rapidly toward their cars. Fin apologizes to me after every pitch, as if he is afraid I could get him fired. I could tell that he is shitting his pants. He is nervous, he says. But he promises to stay positive. He does stay positive the rest of the shift, but his positive attitude kills me.

I give Fin a week to last.

III. Aubrey

Aubrey was the one who oriented me on my first day and was my first field manager before I got reassigned with Aiza. She is a twenty-something no-name actress who has had a few mainstream movie cameos and indie film supporting roles. I know this from hunting her down on IMDb. At work, she tops the "Top Performers of the Week" list almost every week, with the exception of that one week when Aiza did.

Aubrey's IMDb photo belies her true nature. In it, she looks seductive, vulnerable. Her blonde strands fall smoothly across her face, as if a gentle breeze had blown past it. A strap of her dress is down on one shoulder and her lips are puckered slightly. But at the canvassers' headquarters, she is a fiery feminist. She has clashed with Donnie, a closet sexist, on a few occasions, and she is not afraid of getting fired for her beliefs. On the streets, she is the voice of democracy itself. At least she believes she is. And I do think she is. Despite the fact that most of the people who had signed up with her on my orientation day were mostly middle-aged men who made not-so-subtle glances towards Aubrey's cleavage.

But today, she surprised the team by saying that she is quitting. This is a rare moment. Very few people in the company have the privilege of leaving voluntarily. She tells us she found a new gig with a local studio. She does not tell us where this studio is or what kind of films she is working on. We only assume that she is heading for something big, from the way she talked about her new gig. Even Donnie appears genuinely sad, but he does not press her to stay. After all, he knows exactly what this job is supposed to be: a way station for frustrated actors and nameless writers.

While driving to a Trader Joe's in West Hollywood, Fin confirms that, indeed, Aubrey did find herself a new career. A starring role, in fact. He says he saw it once while idling in front of the computer, contemplating whether to send a message to an ex.

"If you're interested in Aubrey's movie, look it up online," Fin says.

Fin hands over his phone to show a video. He is not lying. The first scene opens with Aubrey sprawled in bed, wearing a red, satin nightgown, looking more seductive than her IMDb photo. She is rubbing one leg slowly against the other. Then, she shakes her head gently, causing her blonde-streaked hair to ripple slightly. Moments later, a guy with a hard-on comes into the picture and starts talking dirty.

IV. Aiza

We try to pack ourselves into Marcela's van--me, Fin, Aiza, and several other canvassers assigned to nearby routes in Culver City. There are maybe 12 of us, so I am not able to squeeze in. Seeing this, Aiza tells Marcela that she will drive instead and decides to take me with her.

As we enter the 405, Aiza begins to tell her story. This is the first and only time Aiza revealed anything about herself. And I can tell, from the way she glanced at me at one point, Aiza was amused by the surprised look I gave her as I marveled at her sudden openness.

She and her girlfriend came from Arlington, Texas, where she was born, where she grew up with her parents who had exiled themselves to America after the Marcos regime went down in the EDSA Revolution, and where she got thrown out of the family for loving the wrong sex. Not surprisingly, she is one of the most vocal people among the anti-religion crowd at the canvassers' headquarters.

Aiza also tells me that she lives in a boarding house with her girlfriend. She emphasizes the *girlfriend* in her statement, as if she is seeing through my intentions. One day, she says, she and her *girlfriend* would just bail on America and head out to Amsterdam to live in peace.

When I used to canvass with Aiza, we would spend our break time sparsely trading words while we shared the bread she kept inside her trunk. She always had bread in her trunk. Sometimes, I would bring a can of tuna or some peanut butter, but she would stick with her plain, white bread. She would eat her meal methodically. She would rapidly chew five times before she swallowed. Then, she would take a swig of bottled water. Some nights, we would see a hobo walking around, and Aiza would invite the hobo to sit with us while munching on our bread. We would split the bread with the hobo.

I had always wondered if she talked more outside of work. If she had an opinion about *adobo* and *kare-kare*. If she thought *Boracay* was overrated. If she had ever heard of *Parokya ni Edgar*. And if she'd be interested to hear some of my poems.

I consider asking Aiza about all of these things today, but I don't. I realize that I am content in letting Aiza carry on with her story, in letting it be vastly different from the stories that my ex, Karissa, would tell.

When we arrive at Culver City, Aiza gives me this odd look. Like for an instant we are friends. Then she says goodbye before we each go onto our own separate routes.

I do not see Aiza during the next shift. Never quit, never fired, at least according to Donnie. Perhaps, one day I will run into her again, peanut butter or tuna can in my hand, and she will eat with me with a hobo on our side while we munch on some bread from her trunk.

V. Attorney Lester Noriega

He does his writing at night, especially weekends. He tells me about the piles of rejections on his desk. He talks about said letters with pride, as necessary steps to success.

Before we part ways to go to our assigned canvassing locations, I ask him about his latest project, and he gives an answer so vague and arcane only he can understand. I do not press him for further details.

Instead, I consider telling the Attorney about my poems, the ones I used to reserve only for Karissa, the ones she found so honest and poignant before she realized I was full of shit, the ones I recited to her over shots of pure Jägermeister and several rounds of fucking. But I don't. Time is golden.

The Attorney is on death row, a shift away from getting the axe. Donnie has reminded him during the start-of-shift briefing that he needed to keep up or else. Seeing the Attorney get harassed is surreal--

the Attorney in his business casual attire getting schooled by a boss with ripped jeans and a purple Mohawk. The Attorney is low on cash and contemplates on waiting tables. I tried to suggest that he go back to his law career, but he quickly raised his hand to shut me up. So I didn't push it.

"This is the price of pursuing my dreams," he says. "And I am willing to pay for it."

I pretend to understand the meaning of what he said.

By the end of the night, he tells me he got one person to sign on to a $10/month membership. It is not enough to save his job. Donnie calls the Attorney's attention in a corner. But that doesn't seem to bother him. Instead, he tells Donnie to wait. The Attorney is busy talking to me about this conversation he had with a man from Florida, his old neighbor. He says they were drinking when the man suggested he take up screenwriting.

"I have nothing else to lose," he says.

"Pancreatic Cancer," he adds.

The doctors gave him a year to live.

I tell him I'm sorry to hear what he said.

And then, I wonder if life is really like this--if we only give our lives a chance just before we lose them.

VI. The Wrong House

I get assigned with Fin in this neighborhood in Downtown Los Angeles, which is up on a hill. Donnie tells us we should not have problems in these parts since the people are mostly liberal. The streets are serene, uninfected by the soot and potholes of the city proper. I send Fin away to canvass the other side of the street just to get rid of him.

Two hours in, not one house had opened up to me, although I had seen people peek discreetly from their windows before disappearing.

I take a smoke break at around six pm, four hours into the shift. I meet Fin at a corner. Fin tells me he didn't have much luck either. Just a couple of "interested" people who said they needed to research more on the Internet.

Fin and I get back to work again and this time I decide to take him along with me. After passing a couple more houses without having anybody answer our knocking, we happen upon this one house. The windows are wide open. There is a family inside apparently celebrating something. They are unaware that Fin and I are watching. They are busy talking while sitting around a table with fine China and silken cloth. A roasted chicken is sitting proudly on the tabletop along with other foods I cannot quite make out.

Fin rings the doorbell. We wait. I ring the doorbell a second time. And then, a third and a fourth. After that, we catch the attention of one of the men sitting at the dining table. Fin is desperate right now, but he tries to hide it. He is on his third day of having no sign-ups.

Fin bursts onto his speech immediately after the man opens the door. The man is nice and polite. He listens to Fin's rambling, nodding occasionally to show us he is still listening, or at least pretending to.

When Fin finishes his pitch, two women come to the door to ask what is going on. The man looks at us.

"Sorry guys, but I think you're in the wrong house," he says. Then he points to a sticker on the door.

It says, "McCain-Palin 2008."

VII. The Castle

I am standing outside this really weird house. The design is ancient but the house itself looks new. It is as if the architect had been warped from another time and somehow got a gig designing this house. The house has a medieval theme to it. And, to get to the front door, I realize I have to ascend this really steep staircase.

After fifteen minutes of panting my way through maybe a thousand steps, I come to the front door. I am sweating my balls off. Just then, a dignified looking middle-aged man in a suit opens the door.

"Who are you?" he says.

I tell him I work with the ACLU and that I am here to ask for his support in fighting for gay marriage. He pauses, smirks, and tells me to come inside.

Inside, the house is also medieval in its ambiance, but with a hint of modernity. He tells me to sit in the living room, right in front of a tiny replica of Plato's bust. I stare at it as the man sets himself down.

"We can easily forgive a child who is afraid of the dark; the real tragedy of life is when men are afraid of the light," he says.

I stare at him.

"Plato," he says. "It's a quote from Plato."

I nod.

"We live in very dark times, son," he says.

I nod some more.

He pauses, and then asks, "Do you really believe in what you're doing?"

"Of course, sir," I say.

He calls out a name and several seconds later another man appears from one of the hallways.

"Clay, would you please give this man a check? $500 dollars to the ACLU. And when you're done, maybe you'd like to come listen to what um...what was your name again?"

"Samuel, sir," I say.

"Oh...well pleased meet you Sam, I'm Ronan. And this is Clay, my partner."

Then, Ronan glances back at Clay and nods.

"Nice to meet you, Sam," Clay says with a smile. "Hold on, I will be right back."

While waiting, Ronan tells me he will be signing up for a $200/month platinum membership. And that he will convince Clay to do the same. I tell the man he is giving too much. But inside, I am about to combust.

I am set for the week.

VIII. Dogs

Another day, another neighborhood. It seems that lately Donnie has been putting me and my one-man team of Fin only in the residential routes. I don't know if this is a good thing. I don't mind. The residential routes make me feel a little more important. Like I am, indeed, Paul Revere, riding across town with my pitch that serves as a warning to the American people of the oncoming army of federal and state laws out to slaughter their liberties.

The only thing I don't like about canvassing the neighborhoods are the dogs. I never had a dog, but I had been indifferent to them until I ran into this job. Now, I hate dogs. And even more so, their yuppie, dog-walking owners that had time for jogging and Pilates. You never really realize how fucked up people can be until you are in a position where you are begging them for money, and they are tugging a salivating Pinscher around.

Anyway, I am alone in this neighborhood. Fin called off because he said he caught stomach flu. I arrive at a house where I can see this dog through the screen door. It is one of those cute dogs, the type that gets a million hits on YouTube. I am disgusted.

A middle-aged man is holding a fake bone high up above his head and is telling the dog to go get it. The dog is barking and wagging its tail and, for whatever reason, I imagine Fin's face on the dog. The dog is a 'good boy' because he takes the bone right on cue and finishes with a rollover. He is rewarded with a tickle and a snack.

After watching this nonsense, the man sees me standing by the front door. Suddenly, he gets all tensed up and opens the door angrily. I try to shake his hand. *I am Paul Revere. I am Paul Revere*, I say to myself. But he never shakes my hand.

I begin my pitch, but he holds up his hand two words before I finish the first sentence. He reaches into his back pocket then hands me a dollar.

I take it. I take whatever I can get. I am a good boy like that.

IX. Somehow Make a Living

More people are cut. At the headquarters, the only people I recognize are Fin and this dude from Flatbush, Brooklyn. I am six months into this job. For someone who at one point couldn't even name the Speaker of the House and who just stumbled into this job because nobody else outside the fast-food industry would hire a fool like me, I think I am holding my own quite well.

But my head is due to be cut anytime soon. I know it. This is not paranoia. Ever since I started having more of the residential routes, I have had more days of not getting any sign-ups. I don't know if it's because residential areas are harder to canvass or if it's because California had already made up its mind.

Prop 8 passed; gays can't marry. Obama is president.

In any case, I request Donnie to assign me and Fin to the streets. Fin is doing better than me, but not so spectacularly to earn the title of Field Manager. Donnie gives us the Chinese Theatre down by Hollywood Boulevard.

After battling for a parking spot, Fin and I plant ourselves in the Hollywood Walk of Fame. Batman is close by having a photo shoot with this family of tourists. After a few minutes, the family walks away while glossing over their photos with Batman on their phones. Batman tries to extend a hand for a tip, but the family pays him no attention.

"Fucking cheap tourists," Batman says.

I feel for Batman, so I ask him if he wanted to smoke with me. He nods. I tell Fin I'll be right back. Batman and I head out to a parking lot, away from the people. When I offer my cigarette, Batman waves his hand and reaches into his pocket for a sandwich bag. He looks at it, smells it, and then fishes out some weed. Then, he splits the weed and starts rolling two sticks for the both of us.

Soon, I get high with Batman. I don't notice two hours pass. Fin has already left me three missed calls. Batman, too, realizes that he had wasted so much time and bolts off.

A couple sees him and catches him for a picture. Batman flexes his muscle in a way only the Dark Knight can. He gets five bucks for his troubles.

I stand next to Batman, hoping that his luck would rub off. I manage to get one $10/month sustaining membership from a dude in dreadlocks several minutes later. One more of this and I would make the daily quota.

Batman glances towards me and says, "We've got to make a living somehow."

X. Fin

A changing of the guard is taking place at the Third Street Promenade. The people with the plump fur coats, the ones with the shopping bags, the ones with the latest contraptions from the Apple store are handing over the reins of the Promenade to the hobos and their grocery carts. Somehow, I take comfort with this new company.

Fin is making his pitch to a group of college girls while I sit on a bench, spacing out. He has defied my expectations. He has lasted three months and a week. And so far, he still has a guaranteed job for another week. He gives me a thumbs up and a wink. He is about to have his third sign-up for the day.

The shift will be done in half an hour, and I feel like a terminal patient on a heart monitor who knows the exact minute he will flat line.

Once Fin and I head back to the headquarters for the end-of-shift meeting, I'm sure Donnie will find a way to sugarcoat his way into telling me that I'm fired, just like he did with the Attorney and all the other ones he had fired. Rules are rules. Fall below the minimum daily quota for five days straight and you're cut.

After that, the rest of the night can go in one of two ways. One scenario is that I will smoke until I am too nauseated while thinking about which dead-end job to take next, and whether Eddie, my ex-manager at the fast-food joint where I used to work, would consider taking me back.

The other scenario is that I will pass out for the night with not a care about a damned thing, wake up the next morning, and replay the voice of the man from the weird house.

"We can easily forgive a child who is afraid of the dark; the real tragedy of life is when men are afraid of the light."

And then, without so much a thought, I will stuff my backpack with everything I own--perhaps add a bag of bread, a can of tuna, and a bottle of peanut butter in between the layers of my garments and my reams of unpublished poems--and head out to God knows where.

Amsterdam feels like a good place to start.

THE HILL

the problem has never been
about falling but what
you are about
to fall
into.

I have been to The Hill plenty of times, usually to get away from all the noise of my life. It was the place to be when Karissa and I fought, when my lousy job at The Plaza got too lousy. It was a place to think, to shake the grease and fatigue of my blue-collar job, to share a joint. But this one night, I went to The Hill just to kind of say goodbye because it was about to be closed off to the public.

The Hill was an unremarkable place, a small open canal just over a short concrete wall that marked the cul-de-sac of a suburban street in West Covina. Nobody knew when and how people started coming to The Hill, but the folks over at The Plaza said some fools had wandered drunk into it one night and almost fell off its steep edge.

However, it was discovered, The Hill had become a destination for people like us--the bag boys, the *panaderos*, the fast-food crew of The Plaza, the disillusioned. It was a good place to be. You could pretty much see all of West Covina from there, although there was not much to see--the pink neon sign of the local theater, the pool of suburban houses down below, the strip mall that had a Japanese supermarket and a donut shop, the 10 freeway.

The only problem with The Hill was that there were these punk-ass couples that thought of it as some kind of cheap romantic getaway. Once in a while, I would see some of these fools re-enact the Kama Sutra by the bushes. And they made sounds, too.

Nobody goes to The Hill anymore though. Not too long ago, the city government put a wall to close it off completely to the public. People were not allowed there anymore, although I don't think anyone was ever allowed there anyway.

Thing is, nobody would have messed with The Hill if it had not been for this jackass who jumped off The Hill's edge two weeks ago. Public reaction to his death was spectacular. This fool was in the news for a while, from the local channel to CNN. All sorts of people had their say, from psychoanalysts to pastors, as to what might have led this poor chap to jump off a cliff and let his guts splatter all over the road down below. Me, I just watched it all--day and night--amused at how perplexed people were in their quest to decode this man named Sebastian Zaragoza.

His message seemed pretty clear to me though: he wanted out.

If you had known Basti like I did, you would not be surprised. The guy was something else. He was like nobody like the Filipinos I have met in the eight years I have been in the United States.

Basti was the kind of guy who carried the weight of the world on his shoulders. He was the kind of guy that got worked up on every single detail of life. For those of us who have become numb to all of it, it has always been easy to laugh things off or fuck a random girl until our stresses are erased by our orgasm. But for people like Basti, everything was dead serious. All the time, he spoke about "doing something about it." Whether it was about solving genocide in some godforsaken country or about what he perceived as the general looseness of Americans when it came to sex. I never fully understood how Basti came to be this way, but I think part of the blame goes to the Jesuits, God bless them.

Basti told me that he went to this private Catholic school in Manila. I knew that school. Only rich kids went there. And I remembered as a child I dreamt of studying there (except my family was on a tight budget and I considered myself lucky enough that I was able to go to this low-key private school, thanks to my father's *migradollars*). Anyway, there, at Basti's posh private school, the Jesuits had taught him that he had this innate ability to fly around and change the order of things. Superman style. They taught him that goodness always wins out in the end, and that he was destined for greatness.

That's too bad though. Because what they never taught him was that outside of his little bubble lies a very messed up world, and that the closest thing people could get to seeing change is a fucking dime from some lady at a supermarket while they panhandle themselves out of insanity.

Basti admitted to me once that he had become cynical in America because, according to him, nobody cared about "the real issues." He told me that everybody was too obsessed about pampering their dogs while millions of kids died of hunger across the world. At times, I saw his point, but I felt that there was more to his activist streak than just strong political sensibilities. It was also a way to conceal what he really held inside: bitterness.

See, before I met Basti, before ten women rejected his romantic overtures in rapid succession, before some jackass chick named Patty played an April Fools' Day joke on him and said she was crazy over him when she wasn't, before he started listening to those goddam emo bands, before his parents decided to call it quits and before his father headed out to Maryland to live with the new wife, before he migrated to America and left the first love of his life, Janine--before all that--Basti was a happy kid.

I knew this because I have seen his pictures when he was little. Always smiling and doing all these contortions with his face. He was never satisfied just smiling outright. He always had to go the extra mile and pull his cheeks to maximum stretching capacity or smile until all his teeth were exposed. His eyes, which in their relaxed position were already small, just vanished whenever he would smile. When he was little, he was kind of tubby, too. He looked like an Asian kid about to sing Moshi Anone. Sometimes, his parents would be by his side in the photos I have seen, and they'd be smiling too, looking all satisfied and complacent about life. His father, once beefy and pompous looking (not anymore after the leap to America), played in one of the college basketball leagues in the Philippines. Basti's father would have gone pro had he not made his millions in the tech industry. His mother, classy as Imelda Marcos, light-skinned, slightly brown-haired, and erect in her posture, was a very beautiful woman.

But this kid in the photos was a far cry from the Basti I knew and had to live with. When I met him, he had already changed and had cloistered up in his own world. I would usually see him sulking by his lonesome at some corner of the community college, where I was taking classes here and there but basically going nowhere. When we became sort-of friends, Basti began to join me at parties, but our relationship was essentially transactional. He did not care for my company, or anyone else's. He only tagged along to get fucked up. I was his access to booze, and that was it. He never spoke with anyone whenever I took him out to parties. He would always just sit in a couch or something and get all trashed by himself. Basti was really big on the Patron, which he chased down with Long Island Iced Tea. Very hardcore. Or at least that's what he thought.

According to some people that were also sort-of his friends, Basti had taken Janine's loss pretty hard. But instead of getting over her and living his life to the fullest, like how it's fucking supposed to be, he tried to kill himself on some generic sleeping pills. He survived that bullshit, obviously, but I was told that he never really recovered mentally from the incident.

I had told him many times to take chances. To at least get with somebody even for a night. He never listened to me though. He told me he was no cheap-ass fool. That he was not going to walk around flirting with anyone with a skirt just because. The skirt, by the way, was just a figure of speech. Basti never liked girls with skirts--miniskirts and other tight clothing, to be specific. Basti liked girls in jeans and in other types of boring attire. Girls with heavy make-up were also major turn-offs for him, too. He said he wanted women to look "natural".

"If a girl's really pretty, she doesn't need to spend a ton of time nor money to look pretty," Basti told me one time. Good point, perhaps, but that was probably the reason why he never got anywhere with women. He tends to make every fucking thing a philosophical matter.

When he was doing nothing, like when he was just sitting in class or something, it was hard to tell that anything was amiss. He always came to class showered, and wore nice shirts, cool wrist bands, and fine jeans. He was fit and he had this Asian boy band haircut that he constantly brushed up with his hands. If you didn't know him, your immediate impression of him would be that this kid was hot stuff.

He was kind of attractive, too, (not to sound queer or anything) and I could tell that that one chick in our class was sucking his dick in her mind, from the way she looked at him and all. I would have told Basti about my wonderful observation regarding this girl in class, except the chick was cute and I ended up flirting with her instead. Big, big, big, big, big mistake, though. Don't even ask how it went down. (Basti, if you are reading this right now, you owe me one bro.)

Anyway, like I said, Basti was a poster child. Everything that girls could ever hope to swoon about, at least on the outside. As a matter of fact, the only reason why I started talking to him in the first place was because I mistook him for a really swell dude. I'm sure we have all heard about that jazz that goes "birds of the same feather flock together." And, at least in the beginning, I was the bird that wanted to share the same feathers as Basti.

As time went on, however, he became whinier and whinier when he was with me. He had a blog on Blogger.com, which had a black template and an image of a bleeding rose with fallen petals scattered around it. So very typecast. I tolerated his long-winded posts and even left comments for some time. But he was the kind of guy that if you stuck with him long enough, he would just start to tire and sicken you. He kept a boatload of negative chi with him all the time.

At one point, I just began to avoid him, saying "what's up" in class but did not bother to smoke with him during breaks anymore or to take him out with the boys. But he never stopped following me. He behaved like my fucking shadow until one time, I launched a tirade on him and accused him of being a homo. That really messed him up. So, one day, I felt bad for him and apologized. As recompense, I started inviting him again to the parties my buddies and I went to. He did not come at first, but when he sensed that I was about to alienate him again, he started going. My boys were pretty cool with him and never minded my strange friend, but they barely spoke to him and never actually considered him part of our circle.

"I have no friends. Not anymore. I lost them all back in the Philippines," he told me one day as we were piping through our cigarettes. I've welcomed everything in this country with open arms, but I just keep getting fucked over and over again."

"You're sounding mighty negative dude," I said. "If you don't watch it, that'll kill you."

"Then so be it," he replied.

Basti's common refrain "I've welcomed everything in this country with open arms, but I just keep getting fucked over and over again" still reminds me of that poem he made me read one time. It was called America and it was written by this gay dude from San Francisco named Ginsberck or Ginsbrook or Ginsberg or whatever the fuck it was.

His old friends at the junior college. Yes, he had some. A couple of Filipinos who spent the entire day hanging out by the burger stand inside the community college. Many of them have been in that same college for five, six, seven-plus years and had no degree to show for. They were basically on a tenure track to nowhere. Basti was introduced to the group by Karina and Ada, who had this habit of constantly giggling between themselves. Pretty annoying people if you ask me. Anyway, Karina and Ada were in freshman composition class with Basti during his first semester in college. Probably desperate for company, he approached the two on the second day of class after hearing them speak Tagalog.

"*Mga Pilipino ba kayo*?" he asked them sheepishly.

"*Duh, kaya nga nagtatagalog e*!" Karina said and then went giggle giggle with Ada.

Basti's new "friends" were not all that awful, though. A few of them, I've actually gotten drunk with at parties and such. But somehow, Basti was never satisfied with them. He said that his "friends" did not stimulate his mind enough.

He hung out with them for a few semesters then decided to go AWOL. At first, Karina and Ada tried to go after Basti. But after a while, the two just got tired of chasing him around and left him to become the recluse he wanted to be.

Occasionally, he would run into them in the halls or at the library, and they'd go *kamusta na*?, give him a soft hug, and then move on with their lives. Basti sometimes complained to me that his friends at school just didn't care enough about him. That they were all fake. More than a couple of times, I had told him that he should go check up on his junior college pals, but he would just shrug and say, "They're busy." And maybe they really were. Sitting by the burger stand all day was indeed a very time-consuming business.

"The only real friends I had were my buddies in the Philippines. They were my brothers," Basti often told me.

Basti never broke contact with his Manila friends, of course, but he said that it was never the same without them around. I could also tell they really understood him. They commented heavily on his blog.

Knowing Basti, I knew that it would only be a matter of time before he would decide to pull off the shit that he did. In hindsight, I am actually more surprised that it took him as long as he did to kill himself. I barely saw him anymore during his last few weeks. Missed out on drinking parties. Missed out on his daily blogging routine. And he missed all my calls. For a while, I thought that he had already killed himself or something. I did not care at first and never bothered looking for him. In a way, I wanted him dead, for his own good. But then, I felt guilty one day and drove over to his house.

*

I arrived at his house sometime after lunch and parked my car on the sidewalk. Then, I rang the doorbell, not knowing exactly why I was there or what I was going to say. If he answered the door would I be like, "Oh hey man, glad you're still alive!"? For a moment, I wanted to turn back. As if I was already expecting to a gruesome scene to unfold before my eyes. But instead, I rang the doorbell again. Moments later, there he was, in his jammies and a white tee, looking pretty fucked up but not quite dead yet.

"Hey," I said. "Listen man, this is probably a bad time. But I just wanted to check up on you."

"Yeah, no problem man. I'm alright. Come on in. Want a drink?" he replied.

"Aren't your parents home?"

"Nope."

"Why aren't you at school?"

"I don't feel like going."

He walked me over to his room, while I looked around the house. It was the neatest house on the planet. The leather seats in the living room looked like nobody had sat on them, ever. The mahogany dining table, which was just behind one of the couches, had clear glass top and ornate legs. When I glanced at the ceiling, there was a big chandelier that had like a hundred crystal balls dangling down from it. The floor was neat, too, and did not have roaches like we did at home. There were no shoes on the floor, and I guessed they were tucked neatly in a cabinet or something. The way I could put it was: If you ever came to their house, you would think that you were in some kind of television taping set.

"Dude, this place is beautiful," I said.

"It's terrible," he snapped back, trying to sound all dark and shit as always.

His room was an odd man out compared to the entire house. The guy was a slob. Socks on top of the television. Underwear underneath the bed. Shirts and pants and shorts piled on the floor. One shoe by the bookcase and another shoe across some other parallel universe, perhaps. A bottle of Patron was sitting by his bedside table and I could tell from the smell of the room he had been wasting away again.

"So, what brings you here?" he asked while scratching his toe.

"Don't you think it's a little too early for that?" I asked.

"For what?"

"That thing over there. At least invite someone over if you're gonna get washed."

"Nah."

"OK."

"You want some? I mean, I don't mind sharing with you now."

"I'm good," I said, my body gesturing towards the exit. "Well, I'm glad you're alright, man. I thought something happened to you."

"I just wanted to be alone."

There was an awkward silence. I could have walked out but I didn't. Then, I said, "Hey, so there's this thing at Derek's tonight. Wanna come?"

He stared at me for a long time, as if weighing his options, and then said," No, I'm fine. I'd rather stay." And then he smiled a pathetic smile.

At that point, I lost it. All of a sudden, all the sympathy I had for him just evaporated from my skin.

"You're a fucking sissy you know that?" I said.

"The hell is your problem?" he retorted.

"You're the goddam problem. Quit being a loser. You're in America, *pare*. You just have to live with that."

He didn't respond, and just lay in bed with his eyes closed. Then, he spoke, "Get out."

I stood in front of him for a second, just wanting to give it to him in the jaw, but I took a deep breath and got the hell out of there before I could get violent.

Only later, when I checked my Facebook account while driving to Derek's house did I see his status update that said, "The last nail to my coffin. She's gone. I hope his arms will always keep her warm through the winters of Time." Then, when I searched for Janine's profile, I saw it. There, glaring on top of her news feed for all to see, were the words "In a relationship" and a photo of Janine and some dude I did not know.

I wanted to come to Basti's place again to apologize and all, but I didn't feel like it. So, I just turned up the volume on my car stereo and went on my merry way. When I got to Derek's, I drank a couple of shots and flushed it with beer. Soon enough, I was buzzed and I started messing around with Mara, this chick I had been fooling around with since my girlfriend moved to Arizona.

I danced and smoked pot with Mara for about two hours. Then, I fooled around with her some more before gesturing that I wanted her in bed. She resisted at first, as always, but I knew that it was more of a phony resistance, probably meant to make her feel less guilty for being an accomplice to my infidelity. After a while, when all her defenses were blown away by drugs and sweet talk, I speared her in the back seat of my dilapidated Honda Civic hatchback, the replica of the Filipino flag on my rear-view mirror dangling proudly as the car shook.

"Are you on the pill?" I asked as I banged her from beneath her black tube dress.

"Yes," she moaned.

"OK. Good."

Hours later, I felt vibration inside my pants and checked my phone. Basti. I missed the call once. And then a second time. And then on the third call I finally picked up, totally annoyed.

"I was wondering if I could still come over to Derek's?" he said. He sounded pretty messed up.

I took a deep breath and said, "Sure, man. You know how to get here right?"

"Yes."

After about half an hour, he showed up and one of my buddies said, "There's your little nutcase."

Basti smiled at me and we did a fist bump and then I took him inside. Even in my drunken state, I could still smell the heavy scent of Patron on his skin.

"Jesus, did you clean out the liquor store or what?" I said.

"Almost, but not quite."

I shook my head and left him alone. He grabbed himself a bottle of Heineken and perched himself on a plastic chair.

"Hey there baby," he yelled out to some chick, the girlfriend of some fat tattooed prick who's pretty notorious even among his brothers at Kappa Omicron. Had he been here Basti would have lost his teeth in no time.

When the chick ignored him, Basti came over and reached his arms around her waist. She was like, "What the fuck, get away from me!" but that didn't faze Basti. When I saw that, I felt like I needed to save Basti from himself and pulled him away.

"Dude, what the hell? Do you know who you're messing with?" I asked.

"I'm messing with no one. I'm just having fun. Like you said I should," he replied.

"Goddamit, get your act together."

"It's so easy for you isn't it?"

"The hell are you talking about?"

"Nothing. I'm alright."

"You're not alright. Come on. Let's chat inside."

He stumbled all over himself towards the house, the entire party halted by his little scene making. I was worried for him. Never mind that he was a drunken mess, that was not the point. He just fucked with the Kappa Omicron. And you don't fuck with those boys. Unless I guess you don't care about your life, like Basti.

"Listen up. Hey!" I said, slapping him in the face lightly. "Go home."

He looked at me, then began to cry. At that point, all of the respect I had for him was gone. He blubbered like a tiny little pussy.

"I'm sorry," he said. And then, he just walked away. I followed him to his car, and thought about driving him, but he said he was alright. I didn't push him.

"Get some sleep," I said.

"OK," he said.

And that was the last I heard from him. The ride from his place to Derek's was not that far. You could take the I-10 to get there or just the side streets, but it shouldn't take you more than 15 minutes to travel. But of course, fucked up as he was, somewhere along the ride home, he had enough time to think about doing something so fucked up and went to The Hill, which I had probably told him about in the past.

When I got to The Hill on his final night, there was a whole emergency entourage down on the 10 freeway. The cops, the ambulance, the fire truck. But even they were too late. Basti was already a pile of mush on the freeway. You should have seen the whole thing. It was gruesome.

If you are wondering why I ended up at the scene of the accident, well, like always, I felt guilty. I felt guilty letting him run off like he did and so I went after him. I had no idea where to find him but, luckily, somebody reported on the radio that a dude had jumped off a cliff in West Covina. Somehow, I knew that nobody would think of doing such a thing that night but Basti.

I hung around the area until the paramedics carted Basti's body inside the ambulance. Then, I followed the ambulance to the nearest hospital. I'm telling you, it was gruesome. The paramedics had covered him with a sheet, but his boy band hair showed, and I could see it was all red with blood. The sheet itself was soaked in blood. Commotion was all over the place. From the looks of things, it might have been better if Basti had been beaten up by the Kappa Omicron instead. Basti's mother, who got to the hospital before anyone else did, was acting up like Sisa from *Noli Me Tangere*.

She tried to keep pace with the stretcher, but everyone was in such a rush. When the paramedics got to the entrance of the E.R., they told her to wait outside. The whole time, I just stood there, shitting my pants. And by the time Basti's mother came back to the waiting area, I was gone. Only a few days later, after Basti's mother found my number (the kid left it sticking on their fridge), did I get a call from her asking me a whole bunch of questions.

"Were you with him that night?" *No.* "How long have known him?" *Not very long.* "Why did he kill himself?" *From what I could tell, he did not. It was an accident.*

The funeral was nothing grand. I invited his pals from the community college, just so his soul won't think he was unloved or something. Only a few showed up. Maybe like five of them. Karina and Ada, for the first time in their lives, never giggled throughout the ceremony. But they weren't crying either. It was Basti's mother who was wailing the entire time, the sound of her anguish reverberating loudly through the acoustics of the church. Basti's father also showed up. And, if only for this occasion, his arms were wrapped around Basti's mother as he tried to console her. But he wasn't crying, too. And I wasn't crying.

I never looked at Basti's casket, either. And it's not because I would get emotional or anything like that. I just don't get the idea why anyone would want to look at a dead guy. When my brother died, they had that whole procession too, where everybody lined up to check out the remains, like corpses were some kind of circus attraction. I never looked at my brother, either. I like to look at people when they are breathing.

Besides, I was fine just staring at the photos that were beside Basti's casket. There were a bunch of them, but most of them were photos from his younger days, the ones I told you about, where he was doing all these crazy things with his face.

*

A week after Basti died, I decided to pay The Hill a visit. It was late, but I spent a few hours that

102

night just staring down The Hill. I could almost see Basti there, still lying dead like a swatted insect. I thought about what it may have felt like, if he had lived long enough to feel anything, during the first moment his head bashed with concrete. Then I thought about his soul, if we all had one, and how he had probably sat on the outskirts of heaven, awaiting St. Peter's verdict on whether he deserved to enter the pearly, white gates. Finally, I thought about me, the mortality of this moment, as I stood at the edge of The Hill, one step away from following Basti's fate.

I checked my phone and found that my boy Ronel had left a voice message. He wanted to know if I was down for a session at this hole-in-the-wall bar in Whittier. He knew I hadn't been myself since old Basti died, although he pretended not to notice a thing.

It is true. I was out of it after the kid died. Shit like that can mess anyone up. But it wasn't just Basti though. In the days leading up to his death, I had also been going through some pretty tough shit myself. Karissa had finally decided to give up on me after one of her girls spotted me out in The Heights messing with Mara. I was already on probation when this happened, so none of my "it's not what it looks like, please let me explain" bullshit worked on Karissa.

Don't get me wrong. Mara was no random hook-up. My boys laughed whenever I described her as *mala-diyosa*. But that was what she was, a brown goddess. And the girl had substance, too. Mara was a tough bitch, a U.S.-born *pinay* who clearly carried her parents' native *Waray* blood. She's had to work to help feed her brothers since she was old enough to work. Her father died of cancer when she was three. Her mother, tough as nails at one point, had succumbed to stroke when she was 16. My boy Kenneth told me once that I would get bored with Mara and she was really no more than just a diversion. After all, Karissa and I had been at it for years before Mara showed up. Things get kind of stale when you reach that point. Kenneth also predicted that I would come to my senses and come back to Karissa. But that was where Kenneth was wrong. I never came to my senses.

Even if I did, it was too late to fix things. I was too deep in the shit hole with Mara. Not only because Karissa had found out but because Mara had already fallen in love. Or something like that. I remember telling her once that I loved her too. But I wasn't sure if I had really meant it. Not to say that I was lying, but it can be hard to know how you really feel about somebody when it's the thought of their ass that is bouncing around in your head most of the time.

One time, Mara sat in my car and gave me an ultimatum: Leave her or I'll tell her everything.

For a while, I thought Mara was just blackmailing me. And I directed about a million profanities towards her in my head. But the truth was, Mara had given me plenty of chances to leave her. She had even pushed me away before, saying she was no *puta*. That she did not want to be nobody's little *querida*. I did all the mind tricks in the world to keep my hands off her, but she drove me crazy without even trying. I seriously did not know why, and I wish I did. Otherwise, it would have been easier to justify why I had kept going to bed with her in the first place, why somebody I had just ran across several months ago could make me take a shit on everything Karissa and I had worked on for five years.

Basti knew about Mara too and tried to school me about the importance of loyalty and all that. My stubbornness on the matter pissed him off, but I only told him to fuck off and mind his damn business.

The truth is, I loved Karissa. A lot. But when she moved out to Arizona, Mara had somehow become more of a visible presence. She had always been in my periphery, a regular customer at the joint where Karissa and I worked. But I never gave her any thought. Not that much at least. At least not until this one night, half-passed out at another party at Derek's house, when I ran into her. She was with a friend, one of those *pinays* who dipped their hair in peroxide and had enough American accent to conceal some of their FOB-ness. I originally aimed for the faux-blonde Filipina, but Ronel told me she was off-limits. Kind of like that chick Basti tried to mess with on his last night. So instead, I shot the bull with Mara over a bottle of vodka. And the rest, as they say, was fucking history. No pun intended.

Basti would have killed me if he knew I bombed it with Karissa. That is because Karissa was, in most respects, the kind of girl Basti would have loved. The *Maria Clara* type. The petite *chinita* that looked gorgeous because of--rather than despite of-- her spectacles. Karissa was the sweetest girl, too. She was the kind that would pat a towel on your face after a game, the kind that would burrow her head so perfectly on your shoulders on a dreary night--the kind you'd marry, if you will. Her kind was a rarity in The Plaza, where she used to work too, or any place else I had been, for that matter.

The only thing about her was that she had grown out of wearing jeans, if only because I made not so discreet hints that I wanted to see more skin. And she had lost her flower to me.

We were friends before we hooked up, me and Karissa. Before me, she had been with this dick Craig, some dude that liked to hang around The Plaza late at night with his Evo. I never understood what the hell made her hook up with such an idiot, but whatever. Karissa became my girl after I went through a string of flings that went nowhere, the latest being with this *kolehiyala* from UC Santa Cruz that gave such good blowjobs.

"Hey bro, what's up? You dead or something? Ronel texted.

I thought about calling him back and heading out for a drink. But I didn't want to drink. I wanted to stay exactly where I was that second. At The Hill. I didn't know why, but perhaps I had been looking for some kind of epiphany, some kind of vindictive takeaway insight from what Basti did. But there was none.

Down below, life seemed to have carried on. Cars rolled over the spot where Basti died. The pink neon sign of the theater down by West Covina Westfield Mall blinked and blinked. The I-10 was relatively quiet, except for the Doppler sound of the decked-out Civics and Celicas rushing by.

And that was when it happened. I was not sure what triggered it, and I tried my best not to succumb to them. Tears. Lots of them. Poured out of my eyes against my will. It was the first time I had cried in a long ass while. And for a moment, I hated myself for it. But after a while, I got too tired to resist and I just let the tears fall through even though I was sure I looked like a goddam pussy.

When I kind of got my act together, I decided I had to go. I figured the cops would come soon, probably because of some overly vigilant jack-off who looked out for suspicious cars in the neighborhood. My piece of shit Honda, with its banged-up windows and lowered suspension, fit perfectly with the definition of "suspicious." And it was out sitting by the cul-de-sac.

So then, I decided to go to The Plaza just because there was no other place to go.

*

It was a quarter till eleven when I got there, but the crew was still busy cleaning out the diner. Yolly, the night dishwasher for the last 10 years, whose wrinkled hands were evidence of the effects of strong detergent and power washers, was the first to see me as she was carting out some trash. Usually, *Manong* Lindo would help her out with the trash when he's through cleaning out the chicken fryer and the kitchen floor. But that night, *Manong* Lindo was off. It was Ronel that cleaned the kitchen, and he never did a good job of cleaning the kitchen. Or anything, not even his life.

Me, I was the man of the dining area, and I only worked till six. It was my job to wipe the tables and clean after other people's shit. Literally. Like one time, I had to work overtime because I had to de-clog a bowl full of shit. Some dick had put a bunch of toilet paper in it, and it was I who was assigned to save the day *mano mano*. The people who owned the diner were too stingy to even buy a goddam plunger. That little feat of heroism earned me a gold star employee award some months ago. Which was not a big deal, really. All I got out of it was a dumb photo of my face on the wall above the machine where we clocked in for work. My buddies and I called it the 'Wall of Lame'. The higher-ups promised a little bonus for all gold star awardees, but the promises never happened. Nobody even had an idea what the bonus was, exactly. Maybe the dumb photos were the bonus. For the love of God.

"Foo! Where the fuck were you man?" Ronel screamed from behind the drive-thru menu. He was already halfway through some good Kush and was looking very upset.

"Out," I said.

"Well come on! I'm dying to get out of this shit hole."

I said I was not in the mood, so he scratched his head, shrugged, and took off. Minutes later, Yolly said goodbye and I was alone sitting outside the joint.

The commercial complex was nearly vacant, except for a few folks from the other stores. All the restaurants and shops were closed now, but I could still see some of the employees moving in and out of them with buckets, trash bags, and mops.

Most, if not all, of the people who worked in The Plaza were immigrants. Half arrived in America via the U.S.-Mexico border or through overstayed tourist visas. Every once in a while, one of us would disappear, never to be heard of again. A few, like the hairdresser Lumen, bought a husband for the privilege of being "American." Then there was Karissa, who was sneaked in by her parents from Ilocos Sur on a student visa, hoping a U.S. Citizen in shining armor would take notice of her and take her on a ride to legal status. But instead, I came along--I the Manileno without the proper paperwork--and things just went downhill for her. Karissa's folks threw her out the millisecond they found out about us.

Wang, the guy who owned the Chinese fast-food restaurant, was smoking a cigarette as he scrubbed the windows. I bet he was cursing, because he cursed every time he had to scrub off that graffiti on his window. He had been scrubbing the same piece of graffiti for the last three years that I've worked in The Plaza. His English was rough, but the way he says *fuck this shit* never fails to amuse me.

From a distance, I could see Don Don, the drug addict, in front of the Filipino supermarket with a bunch of punk-types huddled around him. He sold just about anything for 20 dollars. PSPs, iPods, Rolex watches, gold chains, and cocaine. No one really knows how long he's been a staple at The Plaza, but I heard ICE had a warrant for him.

When Sharif saw him, he yelled at Don Don to go away. Sharif owned the liquor store next to the supermarket. Nobody likes him, mostly because he likes to project the image of being an asshole. He really isn't. Or maybe he is. I don't know. All I know is somebody who has had to deal with losing a wife and three kids to a bunch of religious zealots in his home country deserves some slack. Anyway, after tossing a shoe at our resident drug addict, Sharif acted all suave and coy again and restarted his conversation with this thirty-something lady named Aria who always showed up at night in tight skirts and heavy make-up. Whenever she was not talking with Sharif, I would see her strolling The Plaza until a car stopped to pick her up. Then, I wouldn't see her until the following night.

Then there were a couple of guys who were just wasting time, tinkering with their cars in the parking lot. Most of their "babies" were about 200000 miles old, pieced together from junkyards and old stuff from their neighbor's garages. But the guys loved their cars to death. Whatever was left of their salaries after deducting expenses for rent, cigarettes, weed, and wire transfers to their loved ones abroad went into bootleg stereos and mufflers.

One of the guys, Miguel, who worked at the bakery, was playing his car stereo, and my head thumped as T-Pain's drumbeats filled the air. Miguel played loud music every night, but he turned it on full blast whenever we had intruders in our territory. The intruders were the Cerritos crew, pretty boys who splurged all their money on their brand new Evos and Acuras. We never knew, or had the interest to know, where these jackoffs got their money. All we knew was that they would sometimes drag race at the lot near the discount mart, where this pretty chick named Loraine used to work. All of us at The Plaza hated the pretty boys. But no one hated them more than Miguel. He had become the most vocal of the pretty boy haters, although he had not always been this way. At least not until Loraine quit the mini mart and went to college. And at least not until Loraine started showing up at night in a brand new, white Acura.

After a half hour of hanging around the diner with my cigarette, Don Don walked up to the entrance and pulled on the locked glass doors and acted as if he did not see me.

"We're closed. Can't you see?" I said, sarcastically pointing to the door sign.

Don Don responded by asking for a dollar. He was always bumming somebody's dollar.

"Go away, Don," I repeated.

"I need some bus fare," Don Don pleaded.

He placed his palms together and tried to forge a smile. His teeth were all whacked. His smell, evidence of his pious abstinence from showering, was strong even from a few feet away.

"I'm calling the cops. Get the hell outta here."

When he wouldn't go away, I cursed and then fished inside my pocket for money. I gave him a five. Then I invited him for a smoke.

Just then, a car zipped by in front of us and parked next to Miguel's. It was Kenneth. He was our morning shift cook, but he stayed at The Plaza most of the time, tinkering cars with Miguel. That's thing about The Plaza. Everybody hated it, but we still found ourselves hanging out there anyway.

"Bro!" Kenneth called out. He beckoned me to come over. Don Don and I went over.

"I got some good shit from my buddy today," Kenneth said. "Where's Ronel?"

"Don't know. He took off," I replied.

"Well fuck that. Let's go."

I got ready to go, but Kenneth spent the next hour and a half talking about cars with Miguel. I was bored shitless. Normally, at this point, I would have called Basti. He'd ask about a hundred questions about who was going, what we were up to, and so forth before he'd finally go. And then I thought about calling Karissa. But I knew she'd put a restraining order on me if she ever heard my voice again.

So instead, I phoned Ronel to see what he was up to. The fool never slept. You could call him at any hour, and he'd be up. So, I asked him to see if he was still down to for a kick back. Of course, he said he was down, even though he was still a little pissed at me.

It was around one in the morning when we started driving around. Miguel decided to stay behind to keep tinkering with his car. Don Don walked home. Meanwhile, Ronel, Kenneth and I had blackmailed Sharif into giving us free booze by threatening to expose him to his new wife about his nightly dealings with Aria. Aria was Sharif's open secret, and, once in a while, when we did not have any money, we used this information to our benefit. Anyway, we weren't really sure where we were going. Ronel suggested that we wander off to Las Vegas, but I had to work that morning. So, all we did was crash at Ronel's place, which was in this ghetto-ass neighborhood.

By three, we were pretty much fucked up. I was one shot away from passing out while Kenneth continued to talk about Marietta, his ex-baby mama, and about their pending court date for custody of their one-year-old. Meanwhile, Ronel was in his own world, laughing his ass off and spewing some incomprehensible shit about Copa Cabana and Shark Tank investors and his latest love affair. He had been trying to get on the Shark Tank show for about a year now because he wanted to get some capital for this business he'd been trying to start for many years.

"Dude, I don't get it. She's the one who fucked me over and I'm the one who has to put up with her shit," Kenneth said.

"Uhuh," I said.

"Fuck Danica, you guys. I'm the playa here. I'm gonna get my shit together and you'll see...," Ronel said to the wind. "Just you watch. She'll beg me just to let her go down on me."

Danica, Ronel's latest flame, was considering getting back with the ex.

"So, what do you think dude?" Kenneth asked.

"About what?" I asked.

"Marietta."

"Just let her play her game dude. She knows you have the upper hand in court and that's why she's trying to provoke you to do something stupid," I said, not really knowing what else to say.

"Yeah," Kenneth said.

"Let's get out of here. I'm hungry," Ronel complained.

"Yeah, me too," I said. "I need some fucking soup or something."

So, we drove in Ronel's windowless jeep and it was freezing. I could feel my balls shrink and I got this sudden urge to take a major piss.

"Pull over," I said.

Ronel kept driving to God knows where and I told him again to pull over, this time louder.

Kenneth said something about requesting emergency court and how the judge just might grant it considering how much Marietta exercised such "poor judgment" with the baby.

"Dude, who waits for their baby to get a temperature of 102 before they decide to do something?" Kenneth asked. "A lousy mother, that's who."

"Goddamit Ronel, I'm taking a piss outside this truck if you don't pull the fuck over."

Ronel laughed hard and was still in his own world. So, I said fuck it and pulled out my prick. I took a long hard piss along Arrow Highway and I almost fell over the damn truck as I watched my piss make a nice golden contrail out on the road.

"What the--" Ronel yelled, finally coming to his senses, all upset. He pulled over and Kenneth and I laughed our asses off. We heard a police siren in the distance, but we couldn't see cops around.

"Now I need a cigarette," I said. I lit one up just as Ronel started moving again. I almost puked all over his seat but I somehow managed to control myself.

I checked my phone. No calls from Karissa. Normally, she would have called by now, knowing at the back of her mind I was up to no good, but still somehow trusting that I would show the least bit of faithfulness to her. There was, however, a call from Mara, but I was not in the mood to return it.

"Let's hit the strip club," Ronel said.

"Which one?" Kenneth said.

Ronel named this one place where he said he got head one time. I knew that place. Only losers trolled that place. The women were hags, and the customers were people in the midst of a mid-life crisis. You seriously had to be drunk or desperate to go there. And I guess that night, all three of us were both.

"I'm working tomorrow," I said.

"Fuck it. It's already tomorrow," Ronel said.

"Well, what about Derek's?" Kenneth said.

"We're too late for Derek's, foo," Ronel said.

And I knew he was right. After 12, all the good pussies were already taken at Derek's.

Seeing Ronel's point, Kenneth obliged to hit the strip club. I, on the other hand, did not want to go. To the strip club or to Derek's.

I really didn't want to go because A) I owed Derek some money, which I had every intention to pay if I had the fucking money, B) my money issue meant I had nothing to tip my woman at the strip club if we decided to go, and C) for some odd reason, I thought that taking things a little bit easy that night would somehow send a message to Karissa that I was not so bad. That I could get my life straight.

But I went anyway.

I was half-asleep by the time we arrived at the strip club. Some chick led us to a table, and we ordered a round of Jager bombs. I looked like a fool when this tall, slim lady sat on my lap. She had a hand on my crotch and her hair was on half my face. I caught a whiff of her perfume which smelled like something very familiar. Something Karissa might have worn at some point.

Corona, my girl's name, began to gyrate. She slid my hand inside her bra and then came close to my ear to say something seductive, I think. I tried to whisper something back in her ear, but I couldn't even remember what. All I remember was the boner I got. And that I bought her something to drink.

Later, Corona and I went into a private booth. She let me kiss her tits, her belly, her neck, but stopped when my mouth was at the corner of her lips and my hands had wandered close to her pussy.

She asked if I wanted to go into the VIP room. I must have agreed because she named her price and I let her take me to wherever she was going to take me. Kenneth and Ronel were nowhere in sight. I felt my phone vibrate but I let it go into voicemail. Next thing I knew, I was pulling out my credit card and signing a $150 tab to take Corona for a little spin.

Just then, Kenneth showed up and pulled me away from Corona. Kenneth thought, for whatever reason, I was getting ripped off and started to argue with the manager. Then he apologized to Corona and gave her a light tap on the shoulder. But the club guys mistook that touch as harassment and got all pissed off. The manager got two bouncers to grab Kenneth. And two seconds later, he was tossed out of the place like a bag of trash. The bouncers dumped him out on the parking lot just outside the club. People stared at him as I ran to his side.

"I'm calling the cops! You fucking morons!" Kenneth said and then launched a tirade of profanities in Tagalog.

Ronel was nowhere to be found.

I got all diplomatic and started speaking with the club manager. He was cool with me and returned my money. But then he said he was going to ban me and Kenneth from then on.

"I'm calling the fucking cops!" Kenneth repeated, drunk as fuck. I hushed Kenneth and pulled him away from the scene. Ronel was still nowhere to be found.

Kenneth and I ended up buying a pack of cigarettes and smoked about half of it in one sitting while we hunted for Ronel. Finally, Ronel picked up his cell after about 20 missed calls. Kenneth forgot the whole business about calling the cops.

"The fuck were you at?" Kenneth screamed at Ronel. Ronel made up some bullshit that we didn't believe. Years from that night, we--Kenneth and I-- would laugh our asses off about the time our dear friend Ronel ran away.

After this whole drama, we had miraculously managed to stay awake. By then, we were all too wasted to care where we went. But Ronel somehow managed to drive us to Derek's.

It was like 5-ish when we got to Derek's. Derek was out sitting by his porch. Derek himself was too fucked up to recognize me and we did a chest bump and told us to come in his house. By then, everybody had passed out. All over the house, I could smell the scent of puke, pussy, alcohol, and marijuana.

"You guys are too late, man," Derek said.

And, indeed, I was late. Because on a couch lying on some dude's lap was a familiar face that, at first, I could barely make out from my intoxicated eyes.

It was Mara.

I thought about causing a ruckus, but Ronel was quick to stop me. He led me over to Derek's mini bar and popped two beers for us. Ronel and I shot the bull for a little bit, and then I noticed he had already passed out halfway through the bottle. I didn't know where Kenneth was, but I figured he was also knocked out or was smoking pot with Derek.

So, what I did was walk over to the living room, where Mara was, and sat next to her and the dude she was sleeping on. Picture that. You sitting next to your woman while she lay on another man's lap. I felt like a cuckold.

But all this turned me on for some reason and I went over to Mara and tried to grab her. She resisted in her sleep, but I just kept at it. When I made the gesture to carry her, she opened her eyes slightly and showed that she kind of recognized me. I took that as a sign of consent and laid her on the floor. Then, I fucked her in her sleep, just at the foot of the guy she was previously lying on. I must have fell asleep after that since it was the last thing I remembered that night.

That morning, I woke up at about 11:00 with 15 missed calls from my boss, Eddie, but I was too fucked up to call him back. I knew the kind of guy he was. Eddie was a good boss, at least compared to the other bosses in The Plaza, but he wasn't one to be fucked with. No-call, no-shows were just the thing that drove Eddie to give people the axe. But he knew me. And we were cool. So, I thought he'd forgive me if I explained myself wholeheartedly and all.

Anyway, Derek was smirking and shaking his head when he saw I was awake. Ronel was drinking again. Mara was already up. Her clothes were back on and she appeared ready at any given second to smack me in the face as soon as I was ready to feel it. Which she did. And I did feel it. The girl was a hard slapper. And then she took off. I never saw her again.

Ronel told me all about what had happened. But then, he really didn't need to because as soon as he finished his story, I got a message from Karissa. It was a photo of me, butt-naked, lying side by side with an also half-naked Mara on the floor. There were no words, no lengthy, dramatic statements.

Nothing. The photo said it all. Apparently, one of Karissa's girls were at Derek's. And it was that point that I knew things were really over with Karissa. Mara's text came after I saw Karissa's message. It was a longer message containing a litany of curses enough to damn my soul five eternities over.

*

It's been a while since that whole bullshit. And, happily, I managed to live through it. So, what happened since then? Not much. A few weeks after, I quit my job at The Plaza, not out of shame, but because I was just tired of it all. I started not coming to work and my boss, Eddie, got so tired of writing me up and giving me chances that he gave me a dead-end choice: quit or get fired. Karissa, last time I heard, was dating. Kenneth moved to Chicago to live with his old folks. He now works at a warehouse that sold Japanese car parts, which he seems very happy about. Mara now goes to West Coast University to get her nursing degree.

The only person I get to see these days is Ronel, who's been a real trooper. You never really know who your friends are until after you have gone through a sex scandal. We've been taking classes together at the same community college where I met Basti. Once in a while, I would still envision Basti sitting somewhere by himself, dragging himself into deeper and deeper depths of loneliness. Ronel and I are now almost done with our general ed classes and should be going to the state university next semester if things go as planned. The world seemed to have moved on since that night.

But before I completely get ahead of myself, let me just back track a bit and tell you what happened the morning after my little tryst with dear Mara.

Without any thought, I drove directly to The Hill and decided to hang out there for a little while. But when I got there, construction workers were already laying out some bricks for the new wall that was going to close off The Hill to nuts like Basti and to the rest of us. I begged one of the workers to let me in, at least for just five minutes, just to sit there. They would not let me at first, but I pled and pled and pled and then told them I was a close friend of the man that died there. They looked at each other and finally let me through.

So, then I stood at the edge of The Hill one last time. I savored the experience and closed my eyes. At that moment, my mind flashed back to this one night when I first saw Karissa in full make-up and a miniskirt. We were on our way to somebody's party. I was a happy old fuck, and Karissa gave me a smile. I didn't think much about that moment back then but seeing it for the second time in my head made me see it differently. Karissa was looking at me that night with eyes that seemed to want some kind of approval, and I cringed as I remembered what I said next, "Well miss, I'll see you later in bed." Little did I know that that would be the night when things would start to go downhill for us. That was way before Mara, before all the bullshit I put

Karissa through. Since that night, Karissa had changed, not only in her attire, but in the way she walked and talked. She had lost much of the Karissa-ness that made her different. Don't get me wrong, Karissa never lost the demure demeanor she had always had. And she had been a loyal girlfriend to the end. But after being with me for a while, she had shed--along with her long-gone propensity for wearing jeans and tees--something that made me love her unlike any other: her innocence.

Yes, yes. I was the villain. I AM the villain.

After that brief thought about Karissa, everything just blacked out. Suddenly, I found myself in total darkness. Almost all my senses had lost their meaning. Except for my sense of feeling, that part of me which I had drowned out for so long in sex, drugs, alcohol, and denial. I felt a gash of wind on my face. It felt like I was falling, but I could not make out just how deep the pit was or if there was any bottom at all. All I remembered was it had felt so good, like when Karissa and I stuck our heads outside the car window one day as we were driving on the 405, just days after we had hooked up. We weren't going anywhere that day. I couldn't even recall why we were on the road. But I remembered that we were laughing, talking about things that didn't even make any sense. At the time, shit was falling apart at home. My father was rapidly dying of cancer, and my mother was trying to figure out what the hell to do without my father.

But that day was the best moment of my life. Me, Karissa, and a full tank to nowhere.

That last imagery with Karissa was then abruptly disrupted by Basti, that son of a bitch, whose voice I could swear I heard speaking directly into my ear. There was no denying that voice--that nasal voice that was like chalk on a new chalkboard. At first, I heard him talking about random shit. About politics. About his books. About his complaints on life. I was about to shut him up, but then I heard him direct his comments at me and said something that I had once almost clocked him in the face for saying it. Once, while we were arguing, he accused me as one of the culprits as to why love was no longer the beautiful thing he had once believed in. He called me a low life, a thug. A *kanto boy* and a *tambay*.

I opened my eyes that instant. I walked closer to edge of The Hill. Close enough that my next step was death. And, as if summoning Basti's ghost back into my head, I closed my eyes again and said, "You were right, dude. You were right about me."

And with that, I took a step back. Back into the world Basti just left.

<u>DEAR ANTONIO</u>

Dear Antonio,

    Today, I received a voice message from Lucinda. She was no longer asking where you are, unlike her last ten calls. This time, she called just to say that she had given up looking for you, and that she did not need your help with the baby anymore if you don't want to get involved. And she's keeping it, by the way, she said. And it's a boy, if you care to know, she added. From how she sounded, it seemed like she would never call again.

Lucinda sounds mysterious, but she seems like a strong woman, the kind that would not beg for your child support nor your sympathy.

Perhaps, years from now, it wouldn't be Lucinda leaving a message anymore. She probably wouldn't have the time to call you in between her two jobs, in between her two roles as two parents at once.

Perhaps, the call would be from a child, wiser beyond his years, asking you where you are.

That call would be the saddest, because I think I have an idea where you are, judging by the next voicemail that was left for you on my phone. It was somebody who I think is your lawyer from the Public Defender's office. He is asking where you are, why you have not returned any of his calls, and that he wants to help you but can't if you won't let him. Then he pled for you to kindly show up to the local courthouse or else a warrant would be out for you shortly.

Anyway, I just want to let you know that these messages are going to the trash folder today, because my inbox is 95% full, and I have my own messages to wait for. Messages to answer and take accountability for.

Perhaps one of them would be from Karissa, her 15th call since we found out about the whole thing three weeks ago, telling me that she, like Lucinda, can handle raising a baby by herself.

I will then return her call, thanks to you.

From a friend you may never meet,
Sam

CONFESSION

(Originally published by Down in the Dirt
Magazine in 2017)

Today is the day Ronel decided to come clean about the incident at Derek's.

We arrive at the park at five in the afternoon, exactly the time Ronel asked Monina to see him. I position myself beneath a tree, just far enough so that Monina won't see me, but close enough to see what is about to go down.

I am watching Ronel from a distance as he begins to squirm in his seat. He is beside Monina, his entire body weight anchored by an arm on one side. His shoulder is tensed up, stiff as a board. Ronel, the *sanggano,* the one to not be fucked with, is squeamish as a teenage boy asking a girl to the prom. Meanwhile, Monina has her arms crossed. Her expression is bare, as if still undecided whether anger is supposed to be the right emotion to feel at this moment.

Then, Ronel's lips begin to move. I hang tight. So far so good. We had rehearsed everything about this moment—from the timing of his tears to the cadence of his speech. Life at the park continues to remain peaceful. I feel a light breeze blow past my face. Children are running. A mother is calling out to some kid named Felipe, tells him to be careful. I watch the people at the park for several minutes and almost forget about Ronel.

When I look back, Monina is standing. Ronel looks like he had shrunk several inches, while Monina towers like a shadow. I can see Monina steaming. And then, I see Monina slap Ronel. From where I sit, I only hear a tiny click as Monina's hand lands on Ronel's face, but I know Ronel is truly hurt because I see his head ricochet to the side from the impact. He rubs his cheek. He looks up to Monina. He shrinks several inches more. A harsher breeze blows by, causing the leaves from the trees to ruffle a little stronger.

I brace myself. This is where I may come into the scene and be useful.

Knowing Monina, we projected an epic scandal at the park that will rock the children from their swings and make the dogs drop their chew toys. We were not exaggerating in thinking this way. Monina is the patron saint of tormented lovers, destined to one day be *selosa* emeritus of San Gabriel Valley. Ronel told me that once, he had to jimmy the front door to their apartment after he had failed to text her his whereabouts one night.

My purpose of accompanying Ronel today is to save him from the onslaught of Monina's wrath, to be the wheel man that would escort him off the vicinity once Monina goes batshit crazy. Ronel doesn't drive since he wrecked his car and lost his license for DUI. Taking the bus is out of the question, too, because by the time the bus arrives, Monina would have already squashed him into a pole with her car.

But things don't unfold as expected because Monina doesn't do anything more after hitting Ronel. Instead, she sits down next to Ronel and buries her face in her hands. Ronel tries to place a hand on Monina's back, but Monina brushes it off. Fuck off, I read from her lips.

Ronel hangs around for a couple more minutes. Every few seconds, he acts as if he is about to say something, then says nothing. Then, finally, he glances at Monina again, says something, then walks off quietly.

Ronel had come out of "The Talk" relatively unscathed.

Physically, at least, Ronel tells me as I listen to his lamentations at a bar three hour later. The real pain of a woman's anger, he says, hurts most not when she chucks your head with a shoe or when she throws you out of the house. A woman's wrath, Ronel adds, is worst when she chooses to use impenetrable silence as her weapon of choice.

TORO

It was my day-off, the first in two weeks. But I could think of nothing better to do, so I just decided to hang out at the diner. When I arrived, *Tatang* Augie, the day shift janitor, was sitting on one of the tables outside, staring intently at a photograph while he chomped on a greasy burger.

"You know that stuff's bad for you," I said.

"Can you believe it? 15 years in America and I still can't buy myself one of these," *Tatang* Augie replied, still fixated on the picture and not hearing my PSA about the dangers of fast food. "You'd think the American Dream was a little easier to reach.

I stepped closer to him and moved over his shoulders.

"It's pretty," I said.

"Of course. I built that thing with blood and sweat."

We were staring at a house, a brown and white bungalow surrounded by a white steel fence. The house had Spanish-style windows and a small garden patio that had a grotto devoted to the Lady of the Assumption.

"Too bad we had to sell it off."

"How come?"

"Because Lucita thinks we're better off to retire in America."

Unsure how to respond, I just sat beside him and lit a cigarette.

"You know that stuff's bad for you," he said.

"I know."

A few minutes later, Tatang Augie stretched himself and yawned.

"Well, I better get going now. Bus is coming in a few minutes."

"I'll give you a lift."

Tatang Augie shrugged. "OK."

He rents a room with his wife a few blocks from the diner, in a run-down section of town behind another commercial complex. A few days earlier, I passed by that area and saw cops and TV network vans parked across the lot. That night, I watched the news and heard this report: "Police arrested two men in a botched burglary attempt at a retail store in the Inland Empire. The owner of the store was shot and is listed in critical condition."

Tatang Augie, of course, knew about that event but he had a somewhat different reporting style. "He was my neighbor. Good friend of mine. Can't believe someone would do that to him."

When we arrived at his place, there was an old woman sitting at the porch, rocking back and forth on a chair. *Tatang* Augie waved at the old woman, but she didn't look too happy.

"That's my landlord," he told me. "I'm behind rent for two months now."

"I wish I can help," I said.

"Ah, I'm not begging for charity yet. I'll live. You know what they used to call me in our town?"

"What?"

"Toro." *Tatang* Augie flexed his arm and snuffed.

I laughed, but deep inside I felt sad for him.

His arms were soggy, like wet brown bags dangling off a tree branch. His eyes were bloodshot. The Toro was a dying bull.

Tatang Augie thanked me and got off my car.

I drove off, my windows rolled down. Moments later, I heard gunshots in the distance.

CATHERINE LYNN

We do everything together. We love each other. We live in a universe with a population of two. We hear nothing but pure silence even as we stroll the city, hand in hand, in its busiest hours. I could think of no other pair of hands that latched on so perfectly as ours did. Nothing could set us apart.

At least nothing until 5:30 in the morning.

"Five more minutes," I say, as I fumble through my phone's alarm for the snooze button.

I close my eyes, as intently as I could, trying to pick up where things left off with Catherine Lynn. Sometimes it would be in a park. Or in the middle of an empty Times Square. Other times, it would be in the center of Paris with no one else around. Most of the time though, it would be just us beneath the stars, lying down in a vacuum, floating, and quietly breathing in the entirety of the universe.

But no matter how hard I try to recreate the events of our nightly rendezvous, I could never even remember Catherine Lynn's face after 5:30.

*

5:40.

"Are you gonna get that alarm or what?" Laurine asks.

I peer at her then I peer at the clock, then at the ceiling. I do not even know what fucking day it is. Laurine knows I'd rather go back to sleep, but she has no idea why. Is it considered cheating to be with a woman in your dreams? I can just imagine how crazy Laurine would look if she files a divorce and tells the judge I have an imaginary mistress.

Amidst all these thoughts, I get up, brush my teeth, take a good shit, shower, have a few bites out of the toast I burned, kiss Laurine goodbye, then hit the road.

On the way to work, I think of Catherine Lynn. Now that I think about it, we have never had sex. We've never kissed. I don't even know where she's from, where we met, who her parents are, if she had missing teeth. And at least after 5:30, I don't even know what her voice sounds like. It's amazing how little I know about her. Yet every time I see her, I feel intensely intimate. With Catherine Lynn, it is a never-ending first date. Our relationship is like a broken record that keeps on playing the best anthem in the album.

I know what you are thinking. That I am just a guy in a miserable marriage. And all these dreams of another woman are my subconscious mind projecting all my frustrations. Trust me, I have told my buddies about this. And I even told my therapist. They all think they've got it all figured out. But they don't. They just don't fucking get it.

I don't either.

I love Laurine. We have been through hell and back. Mostly, the hell part is due to my stupid ass fucking around, but we have always bounced back. Even when little Raffy left us before he was even born. There are nights when I look at Catherine Lynn and wish that she would just morph into Laurine. But she never does. And it is driving me mad.

*

Suddenly, all I see is a blur. Who knows what really happened? All I hear is a loud bang and the screeching of tires before I felt my head bust through the windshield to God knows where.

The next thing I know, I am lying down in a vacuum, staring up at the stars with a familiar scent and a familiar feel against my arms. It was quiet all around, but it felt like no words needed to be said at that moment. It was just the epitome of a perfect moment.

"Catherine Lynn," I said, not really sure if it was her because she appeared hazy.

"Samuel?" a familiar voice replied.

There were no alarms. I was not sure what time it was but it did not feel like 5:30. I could tell I was in a room I have never been in even though my sight was still blurred. In the background, I could hear the muffled monotone beeping of a heart monitor.

"Samuel, can you hear me? It's Laurine."

ABOUT THE AUTHOR

Raymond is a writer and a licensed healthcare professional. He currently lives with his wife and two children in Upland, California.

www.ingramcontent.com/pod-product-compliance
Lightning Source LLC
Chambersburg PA
CBHW060046150626

46556CB00018BA/2903